PROFESSIONAL SPORTS LEAGUES

NFL

BY TOM GLAVE

CONTENT CONSULTANT
Michael Huyghue
Sports Lawyer
Michael Huyghue & Associates

ABDOBOOKS.COM
Published by Abdo Publishing, a division of ABDO, PO Box 398166, Minneapolis, Minnesota 55439. Copyright © 2021 by Abdo Consulting Group, Inc. International copyrights reserved in all countries. No part of this book may be reproduced in any form without written permission from the publisher. Essential Library™ is a trademark and logo of Abdo Publishing.

Printed in the United States of America, North Mankato, Minnesota.
042020
092020

THIS BOOK CONTAINS RECYCLED MATERIALS

Cover Photos: Greg Trott/AP Images, foreground; Scott Boehm/AP Images, background
Interior Photos: Kevin Terrell/AP Images, 4, 14, 24–25, 36, 44, 50 (background), 54, 60 (background), 62 (background), 65 (background), 66–67, 74, 82, 90–91; Peter Read Miller/AP Images, 5; Ryan Kang/AP Images, 8; Elise Amendola/AP Images, 10; Joe Mahoney/AP Images, 13; NFL Photos/AP Images, 15, 45, 71; AP Images, 17, 22, 25, 37, 50 (foreground), 59; Tom Hevezi/AP Images, 28; Red Line Editorial, 35, 53, 65 (foreground); Harry Cabluck/AP Images, 41; Julie Jacobson/AP Images, 55; Paul Spinelli/AP Images, 60 (foreground); Tony Tomsic/AP Images, 62 (foreground); David J. Phillip/AP Images, 67; Jacob Harris/AP Images, 75; Mary Altaffer/AP Images, 80; Andy Manis/AP Images, 83; Danny Karnik/AP Images, 88; Jeff Roberson/AP Images, 91, 99; Nam Y. Huh/AP Images, 96

Editor: Arnold Ringstad
Series Designer: Dan Peluso

LIBRARY OF CONGRESS CONTROL NUMBER: 2019954182
PUBLISHER'S CATALOGING-IN-PUBLICATION DATA
Names: Glave, Tom, author.
Title: NFL / by Tom Glave
Description: Minneapolis, Minnesota : Abdo Publishing, 2021 | Series: Professional sports leagues | Includes online resources and index.
Identifiers: ISBN 9781532192098 (lib. bdg.) | ISBN 9781532179990 (ebook)
Subjects: LCSH: National Football League Properties, inc.--Juvenile literature. | American football--Juvenile literature. | Professional sports franchises--Juvenile literature. | Sports--United States--History--Juvenile literature.
Classification: DDC 796.33264--dc23

CONTENTS

CHAPTER ONE
This Is the NFL
4

CHAPTER TWO
The League's Origins
14

CHAPTER THREE
The NFL Becomes America's Favorite
24

CHAPTER FOUR
The Playoffs' Greatest Moments
36

CHAPTER FIVE
The Super Bowl
44

CHAPTER SIX
NFL Dynasties
54

CHAPTER SEVEN
Coaching Legends
66

CHAPTER EIGHT
The NFL Draft
74

CHAPTER NINE
Home Sweet Home
82

CHAPTER TEN
NFL Controversies
90

Essential Facts	100	Source Notes	106
Glossary	102	Index	110
Additional Resources	104	About the Author	112

CHAPTER 1
THIS IS THE NFL

As the conference championships kicked off on January 20, 2019, the stakes were high for the four teams vying for a trip to the Super Bowl.

With a trip to Super Bowl LIII on the line, the two National Football League (NFL) conference championship games on Sunday, January 20, 2019, went into overtime. The New Orleans Saints were up against the Los Angeles Rams for the National Football Conference (NFC) championship. The Kansas City Chiefs faced the New England Patriots for the American Football Conference (AFC) title.

It was the first time in NFL history that both championship games went into overtime. In the end, the losing teams would be left frustrated. Saints coach Sean Payton could not do anything from the sidelines as a controversial call from the officials late in the NFC championship cost his team a chance to close out the game. Hours later, all Chiefs quarterback Patrick Mahomes could do was watch from the sideline as the Patriots marched down the field for an overtime touchdown and a trip to the Super Bowl.

IT ALL COMES DOWN TO A KICK

That Sunday had started out well for the Saints. New Orleans jumped to an early 13–0 lead before the Rams battled back. Los Angeles eventually tied the game at 20 with a field goal late in the fourth quarter. The Saints still had time to win the game. Their veteran quarterback, Drew Brees, was driving his team into Rams territory.

He converted one third-down play to keep the drive going before a long pass to Ted Ginn Jr. moved the ball inside the Rams' 15-yard line.

On third down with 1:48 left, Brees sent a pass toward the sideline for receiver Tommylee Lewis. There was a crash before the ball got there. Rams defender Nickell Robey-Coleman hit Lewis's head with his helmet and knocked Lewis off his feet. It should have been a penalty, but none was called. Payton chased after an official begging for a flag. A pass interference penalty would have given the Saints a fresh set of downs deep in Rams territory, providing the chance to win the game with a field goal as time ran out.

Instead they had to kick a field goal with 1:41 left on the clock. That was enough time for Rams quarterback Jared Goff to complete four passes to set up a tying field goal with 15 seconds remaining. The game went

"A TOUGH ONE TO SWALLOW"

Payton talked to the NFL's head of officials right after the game. The official told the Saints coach that the on-field officials missed the pass interference call. "Listen, it's a hard job for [the officials] 'cause it's happening fast," Payton told the media following the game. "But I don't know if there was ever a more obvious pass interference call that—here it is, the NFC Championship Game. So, it's a tough one to swallow."[1] The NFL publicly admitted that its officials missed the call a week later.

An interception by the Rams' John Johnson III helped set up the game-winning kick.

to overtime. NFL overtime rules require a coin flip to see who gets the ball first. Both teams get a possession in the sudden death period unless the team that receives the ball first scores a touchdown.

The Saints got the ball first, but Brees was hit as he let go of a long pass. The wobbly throw was intercepted by Rams defender John Johnson III. All the Rams had to do now was score. They didn't gain much yardage before kicker Greg Zuerlein booted the longest game-winning kick in playoff history. His 57-yard field goal sent the Rams to the Super Bowl.

MAHOMES VS. BRADY

The AFC championship game had similar drama. Mahomes would be named the NFL's most valuable player (MVP) after throwing 50 touchdown passes in his first season as a starter. He battled Tom Brady, New England's veteran quarterback, who'd already won five Super Bowl titles. Brady led the Patriots to a 14–0 halftime lead, but then Mahomes threw three touchdown passes in the second half. His second, tossed to wide-open Damien Williams moments after a Patriot turnover, gave the Chiefs their first lead at 21–17 with eight minutes left in the game.

AFC CONTROVERSY

Controversial calls by the officials are one of the most common topics of discussion and argument for NFL fans. The New England–Kansas City game had some controversial calls, though none were as blatant as the missed call at the end of the Rams-Saints game. In one case, referees used instant replay to rule that New England's Julian Edelman did not touch a punt that looked as though it hit his hands as it bounced past.

The next drive had two more calls seemingly benefit the Patriots. Kansas City lineman Chris Jones was called for roughing the passer, although his swinging arm barely touched Brady. The Chiefs later challenged a Chris Hogan one-handed diving catch that may have been bobbled. Referees called it a catch after reviewing the instant replay. New England went on to score on that drive.

Mahomes had an incredible season, but the veteran Brady lifted the Patriots over Mahomes' Chiefs in the AFC championship.

But the drama was far from over. The Patriots drove for a go-ahead touchdown. The Chiefs immediately countered with a score of their own. Then the Chiefs nearly sealed the win with an interception. However, the turnover was negated by a penalty, giving the Patriots another opportunity. Running back Rex Burkhead scored on a 4-yard run, putting New England back on top 31–28 with 40 seconds left. That was enough time for Mahomes to complete two deep passes to set up Harrison Butker's 39-yard field goal, which sent the game to overtime.

"I thought if we got the chance [in overtime]," Mahomes said, "we'd score."[2]

The Patriots didn't give them a chance. Brady led a 75-yard, 13-play drive to win the game. Brady completed three huge third-and-long passes to keep the overtime drive going. He hit reliable receiver Julian Edelman for gains of 20 and 15 yards before hitting big tight end Rob Gronkowski with a 15-yard pass. The drive was capped by a 2-yard burst from Burkhead into the end zone to win the game.

QBs ON DISPLAY

The quarterback, or QB, holds one of the most important positions on a football team. It's no surprise that the 2019 conference championships featured four of the league's best. Veterans Tom Brady and Drew Brees played the 2018 season at ages 41 and 39, respectively. Their long tenures in the NFL have come with plenty of records, awards, and respect. By 2019, the Patriots had missed the playoffs just once in Brady's 17 seasons as a full-time starter. He had been named the league's most valuable player (MVP) three times and had the most career wins of any quarterback. By 2019, Brees had led the Saints to seven playoffs and one Super Bowl win. He broke the NFL's all-time records for completions and passing yards in 2018. Brady and Brees have each led the league in touchdown passes four times, tying the NFL record.

Patrick Mahomes and Jared Goff are younger players, but the two first-round draft picks had already made strong impressions by 2019. Mahomes led the Chiefs to the best record in the AFC in his first year as a starter. He showed an ability to make difficult throws look easy with his creative play. Goff had an impressive season in his second year as a full-time starter. He threw for 4,688 yards and 32 touchdowns before leading the Rams to Super Bowl LIII.

Brady advanced to his ninth Super Bowl as New England's quarterback. Two weeks later, the Patriots would beat the Rams 13–3 to win their third Super Bowl in five years.

A THRILLING LEAGUE

For 100 years the NFL has given fans exciting plays and fantastic finishes. The league started in 1920 with 14 teams. Since then it has grown to a multibillion-dollar organization with 32 teams and millions of fans worldwide. The two conference championships in January 2019 had everything that makes football the country's favorite sport, including superstar players, drama on and off the field, and plays that keep fans talking.

In the NFL, every week of the 16-game season is important. Hard-hitting teams battle for dominance, showing off their size, speed, skill, and smarts. Games are played in massive stadiums packed with cheering fans. Some of these places are old and filled with meaningful history, while others are modern architectural and technological marvels. There are no sure things in the NFL—any team can win any given game. This is part of what makes the league so exciting for fans. Yet some teams, led by great coaches and players, demonstrate a dominance that lasts for many years, consistently ending up in the playoffs.

The NFL is wildly popular, with teams often selling out many home games in a row. By 2020, the Denver Broncos' sellout streak had been active for 50 years.

The action gets more exciting when the playoffs arrive, as every game is a sudden death step toward the Super Bowl—the biggest American sporting event of the year. The drama and intrigue of players, coaches, and memorable calls add to the on-field and off-field story lines, keeping fans talking about the NFL year-round. Even during the off-season, events such as the NFL Draft add to the discussion and keep die-hard fans invested in their teams. Today, more than a century after it began play, the NFL continues to grow in popularity and excitement.

CHAPTER 2
THE LEAGUE'S ORIGINS

The Canton Bulldogs were one of the teams in the league that eventually became the NFL.

College football was wildly popular in the early 1900s, but professional football was an unorganized mess. Professional and semipro teams were scattered across the country. There was no official rulebook or standings, and there was no way to keep players from changing teams. Most players played for whichever team could pay the most, making player salaries an expensive game for owners.

The owners of four professional teams in Ohio got together on August 20, 1920, in Canton to discuss organizing their football games. They named their group the American Professional Football Conference and agreed on a set of rules. The *Canton Repository* later described the group's goal: "To raise the standard of professional football in every way possible, to eliminate bidding for players between rival clubs and to secure cooperation in the formation of schedules."[1]

On September 17, another meeting was held at the automobile showroom of Ralph Hay, owner of the Canton Bulldogs. Representatives of teams from four states—Ohio, Illinois, Indiana, and New York—were present for the creation of a professional football league. The ten-team group changed its name to the American Professional Football Association (APFA) and named Jim Thorpe, an Olympic gold medalist and popular football player for the Bulldogs, the league's first president.

Joe Carr presents the New York Giants with the league championship trophy in 1934.

THE FIRST GAMES

Four more teams were added to the league before the 1920 APFA season started. The Dayton (Ohio) Triangles beat the visiting Columbus (Ohio) Panhandles 14–0 in the first game between league members on October 3, 1920. Later that day, the Rock Island (Illinois) Independents beat the Muncie (Indiana) Flyers 45–0.

Columbus manager Joe Carr became the league president a year later. Carr further organized the league, creating a constitution and bylaws, restricting player movements, and tracking the league standings. He also created stricter rules to stop the professional teams from using college football players. Under Carr's leadership, the league added more teams and started to expand to bigger cities.

THE NFL IS BORN

One year later, on June 24, 1922, the APFA changed its name. It was now the National Football League. Professional football gained some popularity in November 1925 when University of Illinois All-American halfback Harold "Red" Grange signed with the Chicago Bears. The Bears played the Chicago Cardinals to a scoreless tie in front of 36,000 fans before a road tour took them to games all over the country. A crowd of 73,000 watched Grange and the Bears win in New York.

Grange and his agent asked for more money in 1926, and when the Bears refused, they tried to create their own NFL team in New York. That plan was stopped by other owners, so Grange and his agent started a league called the American Football League. The NFL's first rival lasted one season before shutting down.

The number of teams in the NFL rose and fell as Carr added new franchises and closed struggling ones. The Canton Bulldogs won two league titles, and the Green Bay Packers won three in a row between 1929 and 1931. The next year, a tie sent the NFL in a new direction.

CHAMPIONSHIP FOOTBALL

The Bears and Portsmouth (Ohio) Spartans finished the 1932 season tied for first place. To determine a winner, the NFL added an extra game to determine the league champion. That game was moved to the indoor Chicago Stadium because of snow, and the Bears won 9–0. The following season the league was divided into two divisions, with the winners facing off in a championship game. The Bears won that championship game against the New York Giants.

The NFL was made up almost entirely of white athletes through its early history. There were a few African American players in the 1920s, but none in the early 1940s. Kenny Washington and Woody Strode broke that barrier in 1946 when they signed with the Los Angeles Rams. Today black athletes make up about 70 percent of NFL rosters.[2]

ALL-AMERICAN FOOTBALL CONFERENCE

A group of businessmen formed the All-American Football Conference (AAFC) in 1944 after three other leagues failed to challenge the NFL. The new league tried to form a friendly relationship with the NFL and agreed not to sign players under contract there. The AAFC had eight teams in its first season in 1946, and the Cleveland Browns won the first league championship. Led by coach Paul Brown, the Browns won all four AAFC titles before the league shut down after the 1949 season. NFL commissioner Bert Bell invited three of the franchises—Cleveland, the San Francisco 49ers, and the Baltimore Colts—to join the NFL.

The popularity of professional football grew in the 1950s as games were broadcast on television. In 1950, the Los Angeles Rams became the first NFL team with all their games on television, and the 1951 championship between the Rams and Cleveland Browns was the first nationally televised game.

The 1958 NFL Championship Game between the Baltimore Colts and New York Giants pushed professional football's popularity to another level. The nationally

THE GREATEST GAME EVER PLAYED

A sudden death finish between the Baltimore Colts and New York Giants on December 28, 1958, captivated a national audience. The Giants took a 17–14 lead on Frank Gifford's 15-yard scoring catch in the fourth quarter. The Colts got one more drive at the end of regulation, and quarterback Johnny Unitas moved his team down the field for the game-tying field goal. Three big passes to Raymond Berry set up Steve Myhra's 20-yard field goal. The game went to overtime.

The Giants got the ball first in overtime, but they failed to advance down the field and had to punt. Unitas led the Colts down to the Giants' 8-yard line when suddenly NBC's broadcast went out. A television cable was knocked loose, and the game was off the air for several minutes. The crew hurried to fix the cable, while at the same time a man ran onto the field and was chased by police, delaying the game. Some claim he was an NBC employee trying to buy time to get the exciting game back on the air.

The broadcast came back to see Unitas surprisingly throw a pass to Jim Mutscheller to move the team down to the 1. Fullback Alan Ameche scored—nearly untouched—on the next play to secure a 23–17 win. Seventeen players from the game would one day be inducted into the Pro Football Hall of Fame.

broadcast game is still commonly called the "greatest game ever played."³ It was the first title game to go into overtime. A full crowd at Yankee Stadium and a large home audience saw the Colts win in sudden death behind legendary quarterback Johnny Unitas.

A NEW RIVAL

Lamar Hunt tried more than once to get an NFL franchise. The young businessman finally decided to start his own league instead. He worked with several other millionaires to create the eight-team American Football League (AFL) in 1959. The new league signed a five-year contract to have games televised by ABC, and it started play in September 1960. The NFL responded to the rival by adding teams in Dallas and Minnesota and allowing the Chicago Cardinals to move to Saint Louis, Missouri.

The AFL featured a more exciting brand of football, with more passing and scoring than the established NFL. The AFL added other features still used today, including names on player jerseys, an official game clock on the scoreboard, and the two-point conversion. The leagues competed for fans and players, but the AFL held its own against the more established NFL. The bidding war for players hit a high point in 1965. Teams from both leagues drafted University of Kansas running back Gale Sayers, but he chose to sign with the NFL's Chicago Bears. The AFL's New York Jets signed

Star quarterback George Blanda won two AFL championships with the Houston Oilers. Blanda had a 26-year career in which he played in both the NFL and AFL.

University of Alabama quarterback Joe Namath to a record contract despite interest from NFL teams.

Leaders from both leagues saw the skyrocketing salaries as a problem and held secret meetings to discuss merging the leagues. Hunt and the powerful manager of the NFL's Dallas Cowboys, Tex Schramm, started the discussions, and a merger was announced on June 8, 1966. All 24 teams from the two leagues would continue playing. The winners of each league would meet in a championship game following the 1966 season, but the leagues would continue playing separate seasons through 1969. Starting in 1967, they would hold one combined draft, ending the bidding wars that drove up player salaries. In 1970, they would completely merge, and the AFL would cease to exist.

The NFL's Green Bay Packers won the first two AFL-NFL World Championship Games, the championship that soon became known as the Super Bowl. The AFL's New York Jets and Kansas City Chiefs then each claimed a win before the official merger. The merged league's teams were divided into two conferences. The NFL's Cleveland, Pittsburgh, and Baltimore teams joined with the ten AFL teams to form the American Football Conference.

THE GUARANTEE

"The Jets will win on Sunday. I guarantee it."[4] It was a simple and confident statement from New York Jets quarterback Joe Namath three days before the Super Bowl against the NFL's Baltimore Colts. The team representing the NFL had dominated the first two annual championship games, and the NFL's Colts were 18-point favorites heading into this one. Namath's coach didn't know about the quote until it was all over the newspapers the following day. Namath backed up the promise, leading his team to a 16–7 victory and winning MVP honors.

CHAPTER 3
THE NFL BECOMES AMERICA'S FAVORITE

Commissioner Pete Rozelle has been widely credited with helping turn the NFL into America's most popular professional sports league.

Pete Rozelle became the commissioner of the NFL in 1960, and he remained in that role long after the merger. His leadership helped the NFL continue to grow in popularity and profits, despite the off-field drama of team relocations and player strikes. After leaving a lasting influence on the league, he finally retired in 1989. "He moved the NFL from the back page to the front page," New York Giants owner Wellington Mara said in 1997. "From daytime to prime time."[1]

The new NFL started strong. The 1972 season gave the league one of its most iconic teams. The Miami Dolphins won all 14 of their regular-season games. They continued their winning streak in the playoffs, capping a perfect 17–0 season with a win in Super Bowl VII.

MONDAY NIGHT FOOTBALL

NFL commissioner Pete Rozelle convinced ABC to make a three-year deal to show weekly Monday night games after the merger. The broadcast was called *Monday Night Football*. The broadcast team, including well-known announcer Keith Jackson, commentator Howard Cosell, and former Cowboys quarterback Don Meredith, was sometimes more entertaining than the game. ABC also showed weekly highlights during halftime, a novelty in an age before ESPN and NFL Network showed highlights every day. A record crowd filled Cleveland Stadium and a large national television audience watched during the first Monday night game on September 21, 1970. The Browns beat the visiting New York Jets 31–21, thanks in part to Homer Jones's 94-yard kickoff return to start the second half. Frank Gifford replaced Jackson in 1971, and the trio became broadcasting superstars.

The year before, the Dallas Cowboys had beaten the Dolphins in Super Bowl VI. After the game, Cowboys coach Tom Landry said he didn't know the names of any of Miami's defensive players. This led to a new nickname: the Dolphins' "No-Name Defense."[2] That talented defense helped the Dolphins achieve their perfect season. They recorded two late interceptions to hold off the Steelers in the AFC Championship before getting three more interceptions in the Super Bowl. In 2020, the Dolphins owned the only perfect season in the Super Bowl era.

EXPANSION AND GROWTH

The NFL's modern era saw a growth in the number of teams. The 26-team league of the merger grew to a 32-team league by 2002. This era also included efforts to grow the sport's popularity outside the United States. The San Diego Chargers and Saint Louis Cardinals played the first NFL game outside North America, a 1976 preseason game in Tokyo, Japan. Preseason games were later played in Mexico City in 1978 and London in 1983. Between 1986 and 2005, a series of preseason games known as the American Bowl was held in England, Japan, Canada, Germany, Spain, Ireland, and Australia.

The NFL returned to Mexico City in 2005 for its first-ever regular-season game outside of the United States as Arizona beat the San Francisco 49ers by a score of 31–14 in front

British fans of American football streamed to London's Wembley Stadium to watch the Patriots take on the Buccaneers in 2009.

of more than 103,000 fans.[3] Two years later, more than 80,000 fans saw the Giants beat the Dolphins in the first regular-season game in London.[4] London continued to host at least one NFL game in subsequent years, including a four-game slate in 2019.

The league also attempted to gain a footing overseas with NFL Europe, a developmental league that lasted from 1995 until 2007. It was first named the World League of American Football in 1991, playing two seasons with four international teams and six teams in the United States.

After a two-year hiatus, the league returned with only six international teams. Before NFL Europe closed, it produced a handful of future NFL stars, including Kurt Warner, Jake Delhomme, and Adam Vinatieri.

At home, the NFL grew by adding expansion teams. The Seattle Seahawks and Tampa Bay Buccaneers joined the league in 1976, and the Carolina Panthers and Jacksonville Jaguars were added for the 1995 season. Art Modell moved his franchise from Cleveland to Baltimore in 1996, where they changed their name from the Browns to the Ravens. However, the Browns returned to Cleveland as a new franchise in 1999. The Houston Texans were added in 2002 to even the league's divisions at 16 teams each.

RELOCATIONS

The NFL has seen many of its franchises move to new cities. Oakland Raiders owner Al Davis threatened in 1979 to move his team to Los Angeles when Oakland would not update its stadium. The Los Angeles Coliseum offered a new home for the Raiders, but the NFL owners voted to not allow the move. Davis and the Coliseum sued the league and won in 1982, allowing the Raiders to play in Los Angeles. Los Angeles lost both of its teams in 1995 when the Raiders returned to Oakland and the Rams moved to Saint Louis. The St. Louis Rams replaced the St. Louis Cardinals, who had moved to Phoenix, Arizona, in 1988. The Rams returned

> ### A BAND WITHOUT A TEAM
>
> When the Colts suddenly moved to Indianapolis in 1984, their team headquarters were packed up in the middle of the night. The Colts Marching Band's uniforms were at the cleaners that night and not moved with the team. The band members decided to continue playing in Baltimore, hoping for the day an NFL team would return. The band, created in 1947, changed its name to the Marching Ravens in 1998.

to Los Angeles in 2016, and the Chargers joined them in 2017. Once again, Los Angeles had two NFL teams. The Raiders also moved again, beginning play in Las Vegas, Nevada, in the 2020 season.

Baltimore Colts owner Bob Irsay moved his team to Indianapolis in 1984 without any public announcement after Baltimore refused his request for stadium improvements. Football returned there in 1996 when Modell decided to leave Cleveland because he believed the city did not have the money to build a first-class stadium. The league, Modell, and the city of Cleveland worked out a deal. Modell's team would move to Baltimore, but the name and history of the Browns remained with the city and would be continued by a new franchise in 1999.

Houston Oilers owner Bud Adams also wanted a new stadium. When he couldn't get it, he moved his team to Tennessee. After the 1995 season, the move was announced; it would happen after the 1997 season. But after the announcement, fan support in Houston dropped sharply. The Oilers played some home games in front of tens of thousands of empty seats. In response, the move was pushed up a year. Two seasons into the team's life in Tennessee, their name was changed to the Tennessee Titans, and the NFL retired the name Oilers. The Oilers had been one of the founding members of the AFL.

THE BUSINESS OF FOOTBALL

The NFL makes the majority of its money from deals with television networks that want to show the games. Rozelle understood how important television would be to the success of the league. In 1977 he signed deals with NBC, CBS, and ABC—the three major networks at the time. Over the years, these deals became exceptionally lucrative for the league. The NFL made more than $8 billion on television deals, merchandising, and licensing in 2015, profits that are shared among the 32 teams. The league also allowed games to be streamed on digital platforms like Amazon and Yahoo, allowing more fans to watch games on their cell phones, tablets, or other devices. The NFL entered the 2019 season with games airing on CBS, NBC, Fox, and ESPN. The league announced after Week 1 of the 2019 season that it had seen a 43 percent increase in digital viewership.[5] The league created its own channel, the NFL Network, in

2003, giving fans a 24-hour cable channel dedicated to professional football.

The NFL had several labor disputes over pay, pension benefits, and free agency during Rozelle's term as commissioner. The NFL players brought antitrust lawsuits against the league in the 1970s to fight the "Rozelle Rule," which limited free agency by forcing teams to compensate the other team when signing free agents.

A strike in 1982 shortened the season to nine games, forcing the NFL to use a different playoff format. The strike ended with little change in the agreement between players and team owners. Players went on strike again in 1987, but this time owners hired replacement players and continued the season. The strike lasted 24 days and ended without a new agreement.

That strike was followed by a string of new lawsuits over the next ten years that continued to fight the NFL's limited free agency. The courts struck down the limited free agency plans in 1991 and 1992. Reggie White's class action suit in 1993 led to new negotiations and a collective bargaining agreement that included a salary cap and more open free agency.

A player lockout was imposed by owners during the summer of 2011 until a new collective bargaining agreement was approved, but in July the two sides struck an agreement before the regular-season schedule was compromised.

RIVAL LEAGUES TRY AGAIN

The NFL has been challenged by several rival leagues since its 1970 merger, but none of these rivals lasted long. The first challenge was by the World Football

FAMOUS FAMILIES

Los Angeles Rams linebacker Clay Matthews III comes from a long line of football royalty. The Matthews family has seen seven men from three generations play in the NFL. It started with Clay Matthews Sr., who played in the 1950s, followed by his sons Clay Jr. and Bruce. Clay Jr. was a 1978 first-round pick by Cleveland and played linebacker, while offensive lineman Bruce was a 1983 first-round pick by Houston. They played each other 23 times in their 19-year careers. Clay III, who was a first-round pick by Green Bay in 2009, and his brother Casey, who played for Philadelphia between 2011 and 2014, play linebacker like their father. Bruce's sons also have NFL experience. Kevin played for multiple teams from 2010 to 2014, and Jake was a first-round draft pick by Atlanta in 2014. Both play offensive line like their Hall of Fame father.

The Matthews family is the third with three generations of NFL players. Jim Pyne played in the NFL from 1995 through 2001, following his father George III and grandfather George II. Matt Suhey played for Chicago from 1980 to 1989 after the careers of his father, Steve, and grandfather, Bob Higgins. Many other NFL stars followed their fathers. Hall of Famer Howie Long had two sons, Chris and Kyle, make the NFL. Quarterback brothers Eli and Peyton Manning each won two Super Bowls after their father, Archie, played quarterback for 15 NFL seasons. Punter Craig Colquitt won two championships with the 1970s Steelers and has two punter sons, Dustin and Britton.

League (WFL), which signed away many NFL players. These players included running back Larry Csonka, a star of the undefeated Miami Dolphins team, who signed an agreement with the WFL's Memphis Southmen in 1974 to begin playing with them in 1975. The league played a full season in 1974 but shut down partway through its 1975 season.

The United States Football League (USFL) lasted from 1983 to 1985, playing its games in the spring. College stars such as Herschel Walker and Doug Flutie, as well as future NFL greats Steve Young and Reggie White, started their pro careers with the USFL. The league tried to move its games to the fall and sued the NFL, claiming the league had a monopoly on television deals. The suit failed and the league folded.

The short-lived XFL featured rule changes intended to make the game rougher. These included a race to midfield to get the ball and claim possession at the beginning of the game, rather than using a coin toss. The XFL folded after playing the 2001 season. The Alliance of American Football hoped to be a feeder system for the NFL but lasted less than a season in 2019 because of financial woes and the inability to use younger NFL players on its teams. In 2020, a revived version of the XFL, using fewer gimmicks than before, began play. But the NFL, despite its occasional off-the-field issues, remained the king of professional football.

NFL TEAMS

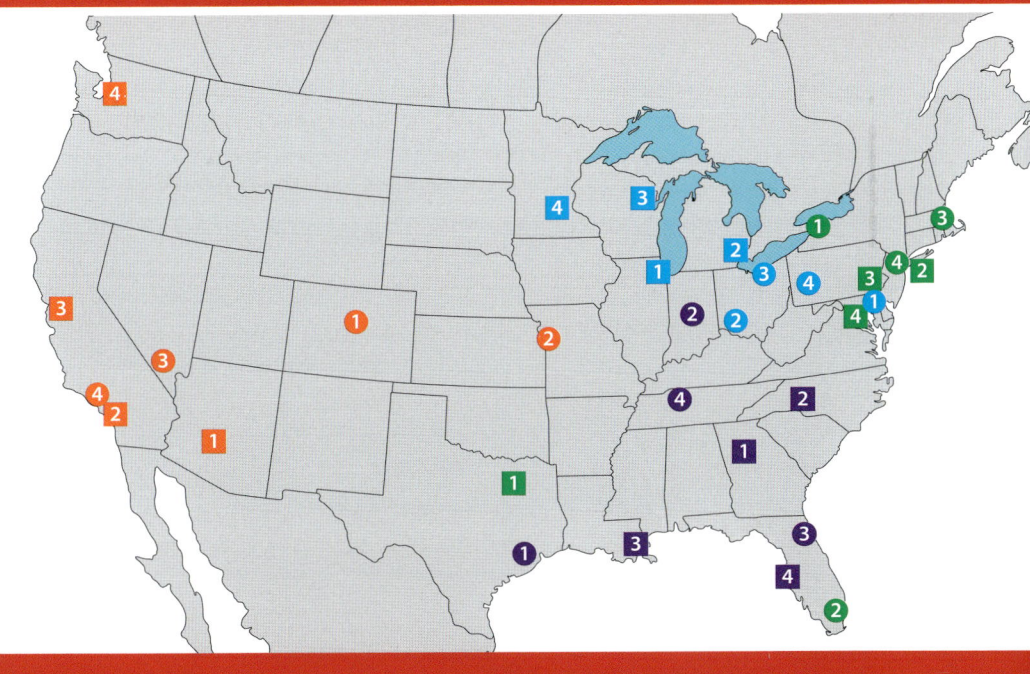

AMERICAN FOOTBALL CONFERENCE

AFC EAST
1. Buffalo Bills
2. Miami Dolphins
3. New England Patriots
4. New York Jets

AFC NORTH
1. Baltimore Ravens
2. Cincinnati Bengals
3. Cleveland Browns
4. Pittsburgh Steelers

AFC SOUTH
1. Houston Texans
2. Indianapolis Colts
3. Jacksonville Jaguars
4. Tennessee Titans

AFC WEST
1. Denver Broncos
2. Kansas City Chiefs
3. Las Vegas Raiders
4. Los Angeles Chargers

NATIONAL FOOTBALL CONFERENCE

NFC EAST
1. Dallas Cowboys
2. New York Giants
3. Philadelphia Eagles
4. Washington Redskins

NFC NORTH
1. Chicago Bears
2. Detroit Lions
3. Green Bay Packers
4. Minnesota Vikings

NFC SOUTH
1. Atlanta Falcons
2. Carolina Panthers
3. New Orleans Saints
4. Tampa Bay Buccaneers

NFC WEST
1. Arizona Cardinals
2. Los Angeles Rams
3. San Francisco 49ers
4. Seattle Seahawks

CHAPTER 4
THE PLAYOFFS' GREATEST MOMENTS

In the famous playoff game known as the Ice Bowl, the players' breath was often visible on the frigid field.

As a football season starts, every NFL team has the same goal: winning the Super Bowl. The first step on that path is winning enough regular-season games to make it to the playoffs. Then the fun begins.

The NFL playoffs feature three weeks of elimination games between the top teams in each conference. Each game brings teams a step closer to the Super Bowl, and the importance of every snap is magnified. The excitement of the playoffs has created some of the greatest moments in NFL history.

FOOTBALL ON CHRISTMAS

The NFL played on Christmas Day for the first time in 1971, holding a pair of divisional playoff games. Dallas scored twice in the second half to pull away from Minnesota 20–12 in the early game. The afternoon matchup of Miami and host Kansas City set a record for the longest game in history. The Dolphins won 27–24 in sudden death overtime of the AFC divisional playoff after 82 minutes and 40 seconds of game time.

The Dolphins tied the game with 1:25 left in regulation, but Kansas City had a chance to win it with a field goal after Ed Podolak's long kickoff return. However, a missed field goal sent the game into overtime. Both teams had chances to score in the first overtime period. Miami blocked a Chiefs field goal attempt, while the Dolphins missed their own field goal try. Finally, Miami kicker Garo Yepremian made a 37-yard field goal midway through the second overtime period to win it. The NFL didn't play on Christmas again until 1989. Since then, several games have been held on the holiday.

The championship game between the NFL and AFL, created as the leagues prepared to merge for the 1970 season, brought a new dynamic to the postseason. The Green Bay Packers, who dominated NFL championship games in the 1960s, won the first Super Bowl. But they needed a wild home victory to reach Super Bowl II the next year.

THE ICE BOWL

A trip to the second Super Bowl would be decided at a freezing Lambeau Field in Green Bay, Wisconsin, on New Year's Eve, 1967. The frigid conditions led to the game's nickname: the Ice Bowl. The temperature was –13 degrees Fahrenheit (–25°C), and the winter wind made it feel like –48 degrees Fahrenheit (–44°C). Packer fans were excited when their team jumped to a 14–0 lead.[1] The lead didn't last, as two Packer fumbles led to 10 points for Dallas. The Cowboys took a 17–14 lead in the fourth quarter, but quarterback Bart Starr led a late-game drive for the Packers. The field was like a sheet of ice, and the Packers were having trouble running the ball. Starr then surprised everyone with a quarterback sneak, running the ball in from the 1-yard line to score the winning points.

"When [Starr] called the play, I knew he would be following me," Packers offensive lineman Jerry Kramer told *Sports Illustrated* in 1968. "That may have been the biggest block I ever made in my life."[2] The Packers would go on to win their second Super Bowl title.

THE IMMACULATE RECEPTION

One of the most famous plays in NFL history happened in the 1972 AFC divisional playoff. Pittsburgh were down to their last play. The Steelers trailed visiting Oakland 7–6 with 22 seconds left, and they faced a fourth-and-10 from their own 40-yard line. Quarterback Terry Bradshaw was nearly sacked on the play, but he somehow escaped and fired a deep pass to John Fuqua in the middle of the field.

Fuqua and Oakland safety Jack Tatum collided as the pass arrived, and the football ricocheted backward toward midfield. The Raiders began celebrating an incomplete pass. They didn't see rookie running back Franco Harris, who was running full speed behind the play, grab the ball out of the air just before it hit the ground. Harris raced down the sideline for an incredible touchdown with five seconds left. The Raiders argued with the officials about who touched the ball on the deflection, but it did no good. Pittsburgh won their first postseason game, and the play became known as the Immaculate Reception. The Steelers would lose a week later to undefeated Miami, but Franco's play signaled the beginning of Pittsburgh's domination of the 1970s.

After his improbable catch, Franco Harris sprinted 60 yards for the winning score.

THE CATCH

Dwight Clark's miraculous catch nine years later started another dynasty and rivals Harris's play atop the list of top moments in league history. The play became known simply as The Catch, and it shares much in common with the Immaculate Reception. Time was running down in a playoff game before an incredible game-winning catch.

San Francisco trailed Dallas 27–21 with five minutes left in the 1981 NFC Championship Game when quarterback Joe Montana and the 49ers started their final drive at their own 11-yard line. The 49ers marched down the field and faced a third-and-3 at the Dallas 6-yard line with 58 seconds left. The next play was supposed to go to receiver Freddie

Solomon, who had made several big plays on the drive, but he slipped as the play started. Montana rolled to the right and had three defenders chasing him down when he released a pass off his back foot. Many thought Montana was throwing the ball away, but Clark rose high in the back of the end zone, seemingly coming from nowhere. He snatched the ball out of the air with his fingertips. The touchdown with 51 seconds left tied the game, and Ray Wersching's extra point gave San Francisco the lead. Soon after, a Dallas fumble sealed the 49ers' first trip to the Super Bowl.

THE MUSIC CITY MIRACLE

A trick play created another iconic playoff moment in 1999. Buffalo led Tennessee 16–15 in the AFC Wild Card game with 16 seconds remaining. The Bills had just kicked a field goal, and they sent a short kickoff to

COWBOYS WIN ON A PRAYER

The Cowboys trailed host Minnesota 14–10 in the final minute of a 1975 NFC divisional playoff game. Future Hall of Fame quarterback Roger Staubach pump-faked before launching a 50-yard pass to Drew Pearson on fourth down. Pearson escaped coverage near the 5-yard line and secured the ball against his leg for the winning touchdown.

"I was kidding around with the writers," Staubach told the *Dallas Morning News* in 2010. "Then they asked [about the throw]. I said, 'I got knocked down on the play. . . . I closed my eyes and said a Hail Mary.'"[3] A Hail Mary is a traditional Catholic prayer. The term *Hail Mary pass* is now used for any last-second desperation throw.

the Titans, hoping to prevent a long return. But the Titans had set up an unusual play in hopes of a last-second miracle. Fullback Lorenzo Neal caught the kickoff and quickly handed it to tight end Frank Wycheck. Wycheck took a few steps to his right, drawing Bills defenders, before stopping and throwing the ball across the field to Kevin Dyson. Dyson raced untouched down the sideline for a 75-yard score for the win. It became known as the Music City Miracle, gaining the name from a nickname for Nashville, Tennessee, where the game was played. Plays like this remind fans that anything can happen in the NFL playoffs.

THE COMEBACK

Some Buffalo fans missed the biggest comeback in NFL history. The host Bills trailed the Houston Oilers 28–3 at halftime of a 1992 AFC Wild Card Game. Warren Moon's four touchdown passes had given the Oilers their huge lead. An interception return for a score early in the third quarter pushed the lead to 32 points, and many fans left.

A successful onside kick sparked Buffalo's rally, and backup quarterback Frank Reich then threw four touchdown passes, three to star receiver Andre Reed. Their 17-yard connection put the Bills ahead 38–35 with three minutes left. Houston tied the game as regulation ended, but an overtime interception set up Steve Christie's 32-yard field goal for a Buffalo victory.

CHAPTER 5
THE SUPER BOWL

The first Super Bowl was held at the Los Angeles Coliseum.

The first planned NFL championship game took place in 1933. But it would take several decades, along with the AFL-NFL merger, for the Super Bowl to become a reality. More than 50 Super Bowls later, the game has become one of the biggest individual sporting events on the planet.

The game became a key discussion point when the details of the merger were being hammered out in the late 1960s. It was decided the new title game should be played in a big stadium at a neutral site. In 1966, NFL commissioner Pete Rozelle worked out a television deal for both CBS and NBC to broadcast the first title game. The leagues called it the AFL-NFL World Championship Game.

The long name became confusing as the leagues further discussed the pending NFL Championship and AFL Championship games ahead of the new

SUPER BOWL NUMBERING

Lamar Hunt is also credited for using Roman numerals to title each Super Bowl, rather than using normal numbers. He thought Roman numerals would give the game a sense of importance. The league wanted to use numbers to track the Super Bowls, rather than naming the games by year, because the game was played in a different year than the season it capped. For example, the Super Bowl to decide the winner of the 2018 season was held in February 2019.

The exception to the naming convention was Super Bowl 50. The Roman numeral for 50 is L, but the NFL didn't like the look of "Super Bowl L." It instead used the number 50 and switched back to Roman numerals a year later.

title game. Kansas City owner Lamar Hunt used a different name in one meeting: the Super Bowl. Hunt thought of the name on the fly, probably inspired by a rubber ball, called a Super Ball, that his kids were playing with at the time. The media used the name Super Bowl for the first few championships. It was first used officially for Super Bowl III. "I guess it is a little corny," Hunt told the *St. Petersburg Times* in 1970. "But it looks like we're stuck with it."[1]

WATCHING THE BIG GAME

Super Bowl I reached 51.2 million television viewers. The NFL's signature game, which is the only one-game winner-take-all championship among major US professional sports, hit more than 100 million viewers for the first time at Super Bowl XLIV in 2010. By 2019, the top ratings were still for Super Bowl XLIX on February 1, 2015, when 114.4 million people tuned in to see New England defeat Seattle.[2]

With all those eyeballs glued to a television on Super Bowl Sunday, companies pay a lot of money to get their commercials shown during the game. Commercials for Super Bowl I cost between $37,500 and $42,500.[3] That number has skyrocketed. A 30-second ad in 2002 cost $2.3 million. That price had jumped to more than $5 million by 2019.[4] Commercials have become a huge part of the game as companies try to impress and surprise with creative and memorable advertisements.

The halftime show of the Super Bowl has also grown from humble beginnings to its own phenomenon. The earliest games featured college or high school marching bands and drill teams. The NFL finally realized the halftime show could be a major attraction for television viewers. Super Bowl XXV in 1991 was the first to feature a pop music group in New Kids on the Block. However, many point to Michael Jackson's performance at Super Bowl XXVII two years later as pushing the halftime show to its current status as a showcase for superstars.

SUPER MOMENTS

The biggest game of the year has featured some of football's biggest moments. Running back John Riggins, nicknamed The Diesel, had 98 carries in three playoff games to lead Washington to Super Bowl XVII. He rushed another 38 times there, none bigger than a 43-yard go-ahead touchdown run on fourth-and-1 in the fourth quarter.

Sometimes it's a surprise touchdown that stands out in the Super Bowl. Rookie defensive lineman William "The Refrigerator" Perry was used as a running back in Chicago's lopsided Super Bowl XX win against New England, bulldozing into the end zone for a 1-yard score late in the game.

Quarterback Joe Montana sent San Francisco coach Bill Walsh to retirement by leading a 92-yard game-winning drive in Super Bowl XXIII. Montana hit John Taylor in the back of the end zone with 34 seconds left to defeat Cincinnati. It was the third Super Bowl for both Montana and Walsh.

Denver quarterback John Elway had lost three Super Bowls heading into Super Bowl XXXII, and he was determined to get his first title. The Broncos were tied with Green Bay late in the third quarter and faced a third-and-6 at the Packer 12 when Elway took off. The 37-year-old sprinted down the field toward a first down and dove as he met three defenders. They sent him spinning in midair

TURF TROUBLE

Rookie kicker Jim O'Brien hit a 32-yard field goal with five seconds left in Super Bowl V to give the Baltimore Colts a win over Dallas. It was no sure shot, as O'Brien was uncomfortable with the playing surface at the Orange Bowl in Miami. It was the first Super Bowl played on artificial turf. The Colts tied the game early when tight end John Mackey caught a tipped pass from Johnny Unitas and raced 75 yards for a score. O'Brien missed the ensuing extra point attempt. Two late interceptions helped the Colts rally again and set up O'Brien's game-winner.

Legend has it that O'Brien was so nervous before his kick that he tried to pick up some blades of grass to gauge the wind, but then realized he couldn't because it was artificial turf. Colts quarterback and holder Earl Morrall tells a different version of the story. Teammates were trying to break the tension and joked with O'Brien about testing the wind. "We kidded Jim," Morrall told the *Palm Beach Post* in 2010. "We were counting on him, but he wasn't nervous."[5] Either way, the kick was good, and O'Brien leaped into the air to celebrate his Super Bowl success.

MINI BIOGRAPHY

JOE MONTANA

Joe Montana built a reputation of being cool under pressure, helping lead his teams to 31 fourth-quarter comebacks. The Catch wasn't his first example of late-game heroics. Montana led the University of Notre Dame to five comebacks during his college career, which included the 1977 National Championship. In his final game with the Irish, he needed hot chicken soup to fight off chills before erasing a 22-point deficit against Houston in the 1979 Cotton Bowl. Montana was chosen in the third round of that year's NFL Draft. He led the 49ers to four Super Bowl wins in the next ten years. He was the Super Bowl MVP for three of those victories. After missing nearly two years due to injury, Montana was traded to Kansas City and played two years there before retiring in 1994. His Number 16 jersey was retired by San Francisco in 1997, and he was inducted into the Pro Football Hall of Fame in 2000.

◄ Montana prepares to throw a pass in Super Bowl XVI.

like a helicopter, but Elway got enough yards for the first down. He landed, smiled, and led his team to a go-ahead touchdown. Elway's determination would propel the Broncos to a 31–24 win.

Tennessee receiver Kevin Dyson had the same determination in Super Bowl XXXIV but came up a yard short against the Saint Louis Rams. The Titans rallied from a 16–0 deficit to tie the game in the fourth quarter, only to see the Rams answer with a 73-yard touchdown from Kurt Warner to Isaac Bruce. With 1:54 remaining, Titans quarterback Steve McNair marched his team down the field. On the final play of the game, McNair hit Dyson over the middle. But the receiver was just short of the end zone. Rams linebacker Mike Jones arrived right after the ball did, and he wrestled Dyson to the ground as the receiver stretched his hand and the ball, coming up just inches short of the goal line.

SUPER PATRIOTS

Tom Brady won his sixth title in Super Bowl LIII. Many trips to the championship game have seen big Patriot moments. One, however, went against New England. The Patriots entered Super Bowl XLII after going 16–0 in the 2007 regular season. A victory would let them join Miami's 1972 team as the only undefeated Super Bowl champions. The Patriots led late in the game, but the New York Giants spoiled history as Eli Manning escaped heavy pressure on third down and hit receiver David Tyree. Tyree leaped into the air and somehow caught the ball, pinning it between one hand and his helmet. Manning hit Plaxico Burress for a go-ahead score a few plays later.

Nearly a decade later, Brady led the Patriots to the biggest comeback in Super Bowl history. New England trailed Atlanta 28–3 in the third quarter of Super Bowl LI before Brady led his team on four consecutive scoring drives to force the first overtime in Super Bowl history. The game-tying drive included an incredible catch by Julian Edelman, who grabbed a deflected ball that was literally inches from hitting the ground. James White's touchdown run with a minute left tied it, and his overtime score gave New England another Super Bowl victory.

SUPER BROTHERS

Baltimore's John Harbaugh and San Francisco's Jim Harbaugh became the first brothers to square off as head coaches in a Super Bowl when they met at Super Bowl XLVII in February 2013. The brothers also faced off on Thanksgiving Day 2011. John and the Ravens won both meetings, including a 34–31 win at the "HarBowl."

Twin brothers Jason and Devin McCourty became the first twins to play in a Super Bowl when New England won Super Bowl LIII in February 2019. Devin was drafted by the Patriots in 2010, and Jason joined him there after a 2018 trade.

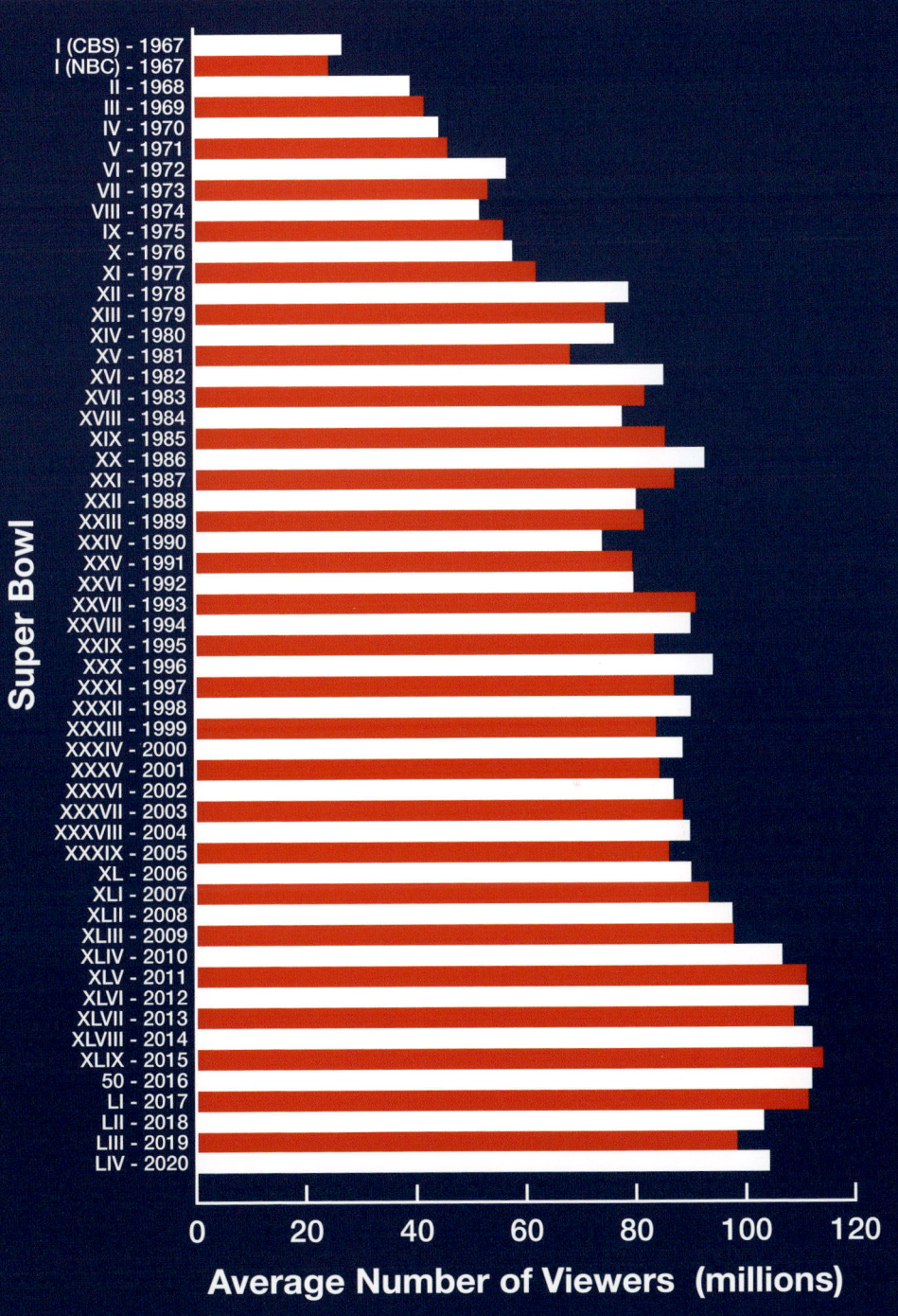

CHAPTER 6
NFL DYNASTIES

Coach Bill Belichick and quarterback Tom Brady have worked together to create the greatest dynasty in the history of the NFL. ▶

The New England Patriots were regulars in the postseason between 2001 and 2019. In that span of 19 seasons, behind the leadership of coach Bill Belichick and quarterback Tom Brady, the Patriots won their AFC East Division 17 times. Those 17 postseason appearances included nine trips to the Super Bowl. Brady, Belichick, and the Patriots won six of those Super Bowls.

Long periods of domination are not unprecedented in the NFL, but to have a dynasty last nearly two decades certainly puts the franchise at the top of the league's history books. It started simply enough. In 2001, Belichick was the Patriots' second-year coach and Brady was a second-year backup quarterback who replaced injured starter Drew Bledsoe early in the season. Brady went 12–3 as a starter before Bledsoe helped the Patriots upset Pittsburgh in the playoffs after Brady sprained his ankle. Brady returned to start Super Bowl XXXVI and led a late drive to set up Adam Vinatieri's 48-yard field goal as time expired for the win.

It was the first of three Super Bowl victories in a four-year span for the Patriots. Only the Dallas Cowboys had done that before. Brady, Belichick, and a few assistant coaches are the only members of the Patriots to participate in all six Super Bowl victories. The Patriots won three more Super Bowls, XLIX, LI, and LIII, making them the second franchise with six titles. The Patriots' dynasty is only the latest in a long history of dominant NFL teams.

PRE-MERGER DYNASTIES

The Green Bay Packers are the NFL's original dynasty. They won three straight league championships between 1929 and 1931. They then won three more titles between 1936 and 1944 behind record-setting receiver Don Hutson after the addition of a title game.

The Cleveland Browns dominated the All-American Football Conference, winning all four of the league's titles before it folded in 1949. The Browns' success continued when they joined the NFL. They played in six straight championship games and won three between 1950 and 1955. Quarterback Otto Graham was a key playmaker for the Browns, leading the NFL in passing in many of those championship seasons.

The Packers returned to prominence in the 1960s. They won three NFL titles and the first two Super Bowls in a seven-year period. Coach Vince Lombardi and quarterback

LOMBARDI'S PROMISE

Vince Lombardi led Green Bay to the NFL Championship Game in his second season, but the Packers lost that 1960 title to Philadelphia 17–13. The Packers were driving the ball deep in Eagle territory when time expired. In the locker room after the disappointing loss, Lombardi promised to never lose another title game. "I've always remembered Vince's speech," Packers running back Paul Hornung told the *New York Times* in 2011. "He told us, 'We'll never lose another championship.' And we didn't."[1] Green Bay would win five titles in a seven-year span under Lombardi.

Bart Starr were at the center of those championship teams, going 9–1 in the playoffs.

THE STEELERS IN THE 1970s

Coach Chuck Noll led the Steelers to four Super Bowl wins in a six-year span as Pittsburgh suddenly dominated the 1970s after years of struggling. The Steelers won the AFC Central seven times and went to the playoffs eight straight years

THREE TITLES, THREE QBs

The Washington Redskins put together a successful run between 1982 and 1992, making the playoffs eight times and winning three Super Bowls. Joe Gibbs became the only coach in NFL history to win three Super Bowls with three different quarterbacks. Joe Theismann spent four years with Washington before becoming the full-time starter in 1978. His best seasons were the strike-shortened 1982 season, when the Redskins won Super Bowl XVII, and 1983, when the Redskins lost the Super Bowl to the Raiders.

Doug Williams was the first black quarterback to play in a Super Bowl, and he won MVP honors after throwing four touchdown passes in the Super Bowl XXII victory. Williams had been a backup until he led a late-game comeback in the regular-season finale and earned the starting job for the playoff run.

In Super Bowl XXVI, the Buffalo Bills wanted to focus on stopping the run and forcing Redskins quarterback Mark Rypien to beat them. Rypien did just that, throwing for 292 yards and two touchdowns to win the game. Among the three, only Theismann missed out on being named Super Bowl MVP. That honor went to running back John Riggins at Super Bowl XVII after his 43-yard game-winning touchdown run.

Cleveland Browns quarterback Otto Graham lunges forward for a touchdown in the 1955 NFL championship game.

MINI BIOGRAPHY

JERRY RICE

Jerry Rice didn't start playing football until he was a high school sophomore in Mississippi. He wasn't recruited by major colleges but went on to become a record-setting receiver at Mississippi Valley State before becoming a record-setting receiver in the NFL. Rice set several Division I-AA records during his senior season and caught the eye of San Francisco coach Bill Walsh. San Francisco drafted Rice in the first round of the 1985 NFL Draft. Rice had a breakout year in 1987 with a record 22 touchdown catches. He is considered one of the best receivers in history after leading the league in receiving yards and touchdowns six times apiece during his 20-season career. Rice added 22 touchdowns in 29 playoff games, including eight Super Bowl touchdowns, as he helped the 49ers win three titles. Rice, who also has the most total touchdowns in NFL history with 208, was inducted into the Pro Football Hall of Fame in 2010.

◂ Rice grabs a catch in his rookie season in a game against the Giants.

behind quarterback Terry Bradshaw and the intimidating defense known as the Steel Curtain.

Bradshaw led a high-scoring offense. He was named the NFL MVP in 1978 and won two Super Bowl MVP awards. Defensive linemen L. C. Greenwood, Joe Greene, Dwight White, and Ernie Holmes started along the defensive line, while intimidating linebackers Jack Ham and Jack Lambert and dynamic cornerback Mel Blount helped form a dominant back seven. Lambert and Greene each received accolades as the NFL's Defensive Player of the Year during Pittsburgh's dynasty. Franco Harris's Immaculate Reception gave the Steelers their first-ever playoff win in 1972, and they won the Super Bowl two seasons later. Pittsburgh became the first team to win four Super Bowls and the only team to win back-to-back titles on two different occasions.

THE 49ERS IN THE 1980s

San Francisco put together a long successful run thanks to a handful of Hall of Famers, including two quarterbacks, a wide receiver, and a head coach. The 49ers drafted Joe Montana in 1979, and he and head coach Bill Walsh led the 49ers to their first Super Bowl win three seasons later to start their dynasty. That first title run, in which they beat Cincinnati in Super Bowl XVI, was highlighted by The Catch.

Montana led the 49ers to a 15–1 regular-season record in 1984 on the way to their second Super Bowl win.

MINI BIOGRAPHY

EMMITT SMITH

Most scouts thought Emmitt Smith was too small and too slow to play professional football. Despite being named the national player of the year by two magazines as a high school senior in Florida and an All-American at the University of Florida, many were surprised when Dallas picked him in the first round of the 1990 NFL Draft.

Smith spent his years in Dallas proving everyone wrong. He led the NFL in rushing four times and rushed for more than 1,000 yards in 11 consecutive seasons. The Cowboys won three Super Bowls in four years with Smith, and he was named 1993 NFL MVP and Super Bowl XXVIII MVP in the same season. Smith broke his idol Walter Payton's record of career rushing yards in 2002 and finished his career with 18,355. Smith spent two seasons in Arizona before retiring in 2004.

Smith showed great durability, playing for 15 seasons in the NFL.

The addition of receiver Jerry Rice turned the 49ers into one of the best offensive teams for the next decade, and San Francisco won a third title on Montana's late drive in Walsh's final game.

The 49ers repeated under new coach George Seifert, using their league-leading offense and great defense to blow out Denver in Super Bowl XXIV. An injury to Montana during the 1991 season opened the door for backup quarterback Steve Young, who led the 49ers to their fifth Super Bowl after the 1994 season. Montana and Young each won NFL MVP honors twice, and Rice became the league's all-time greatest receiver, leading the NFL in receiving yards and touchdown catches six different times. The 49ers won their division 13 times and made the playoffs 16 times in a remarkable 18-year span. They might have won more Super Bowls if they hadn't run into another great team in the 1990s.

THE COWBOYS IN THE 1990s

The Dallas Cowboys, led by the offensive trio of quarterback Troy Aikman, running back Emmitt Smith, and receiver Michael Irving, battled the 49ers for supremacy in the 1990s. The Cowboys won the NFC East Division five straight times on the way to six consecutive playoff appearances, leading to three Super Bowl victories in a four-year span.

The Triplets, as they were called, led the Cowboys to back-to-back championships, beating Buffalo in Super Bowls XXVII and XXVIII. Aikman and Smith were named Super Bowl MVPs. A coaching change and a loss to San Francisco in the NFC Championship Game prevented a third straight Super Bowl victory, but the Cowboys returned to win Super Bowl XXX and a historic third title. Cowboys defender Larry Brown was named MVP after his two interceptions set up two Smith touchdowns against Pittsburgh.

MULTIPLE SUPER BOWL WINS

The Raiders won three Super Bowls in a 12-year span that included two coaches and several quarterbacks. Coach John Madden led the Raiders to six straight playoff appearances and a win in Super Bowl XI. Quarterback Ken Stabler directed some of the league's top offenses during those seasons. Coach Tom Flores and quarterback Jim Plunkett then teamed to win Super Bowls XV and XVIII.

The Miami Dolphins' strong offense led them to four straight AFC East Division titles, three straight Super Bowl appearances, and back-to-back championships in the early 1970s. Dolphins running back Larry Csonka recorded a 1,000-yard season in 1973 and had two touchdowns in Super Bowl VIII.

ALL-TIME LEADERS

PASSING TOUCHDOWNS

1. Drew **BREES**
2. Tom **BRADY**
3. Peyton **MANNING**
4. Brett **FAVRE**
5. Dan **MARINO**

RUSHING TOUCHDOWNS

1. Emmitt **SMITH**
2. LaDainian **TOMLINSON**
3. Marcus **ALLEN**
4. Adrian **PETERSON**
5. Walter **PAYTON**

RECEIVING TOUCHDOWNS

1. Jerry **RICE**
2. Randy **MOSS**
3. Terrell **OWENS**
4. Cris **CARTER**
5. Marvin **HARRISON**

POINTS SCORED

1. Adam **VINATIERI**
2. Morten **ANDERSEN**
3. Gary **ANDERSON**
4. Jason **HANSON**
5. John **CARNEY**

CHAPTER 7
COACHING LEGENDS

Belichick spent more than a decade as an assistant coach before he got a chance to be the head coach of an NFL team. ▶

The New England dynasty didn't start until quarterback Tom Brady started playing for coach Bill Belichick. Belichick had been in the NFL for a long time when he was hired by the Patriots in 2000. He started out of college with the Baltimore Colts in 1975 and worked his way through different jobs before becoming the defensive coordinator for the New York Giants under coach Bill Parcells in 1985.

Belichick later became Cleveland's head coach for five years before returning to work under Parcells for another four years with the Patriots and New York Jets. Belichick was named Parcells's successor with the Jets in 1999, but he decided to get out of his mentor's shadow and went to New England instead. The rest is history—19 straight winning seasons between 2001 and 2019, 17 division titles, and six Super Bowl wins. His sixth Super Bowl win after the 2018 season tied him with greats George Halas and Curly Lambeau as the only coaches with six NFL championships.

Belichick, known to be brash, detail-oriented, and hard on his players and staff, was influenced by his father, who was a longtime college football assistant and scout, and Parcells. Parcells won two Super Bowls with the Giants and led three other teams to the playoffs during his Hall of Fame career. Several other former Parcells assistants went on to be NFL head coaches, including Sean Payton and Tom Coughlin.

EARLY GREATS

Halas, Lambeau, Vince Lombardi, and Guy Chamberlin stand among the top coaches in early NFL history. Chamberlin was a player-coach with three different teams in the 1920s and won four league titles. Halas was a player-coach for the Chicago Bears, racking up 318 wins and six NFL titles in a 40-year career. Lambeau founded the Green Bay Packers in 1921 and served as a player-coach, leading the first Packer

MINORITY COACHES

Fritz Pollard was one of two African American players when the American Professional Football Association was created in 1920. He led the Akron (Ohio) Pros to the league's first title and was named a co-coach of the Pros the next year. He played for—and sometimes coached—several other teams in the 1920s.

Pollard was the only minority coach in the NFL's history until Oakland hired Tom Flores in 1979. Flores was the first Hispanic quarterback in professional football history when he played for the Raiders in the 1960s, and he later won a Super Bowl title as a backup in Kansas City. Flores returned to the Raiders as an assistant coach under John Madden before replacing Madden as head coach. Flores was the first minority coach to win a Super Bowl and the first person to win a Super Bowl as a player, assistant coach, and head coach. Flores later became president and general manager for the Seattle Seahawks, breaking another racial barrier in the front office.

Art Shell was hired by Oakland in 1989, becoming the league's second African American head coach. It would take another 17 years before an African American head coach made it to the Super Bowl. Chicago's Lovie Smith and Indianapolis's Tony Dungy both led their teams to Super Bowl XLI, with Dungy being the first African American head coach to lift the Lombardi Trophy.

dynasty to six titles. Lombardi oversaw the next Packer dynasty, winning three NFL titles before the merger, as well as the first two Super Bowls.

Defensive-minded Lombardi and offensive-minded Tom Landry worked together as coordinators with the New York Giants from 1954 to 1958 before getting their first head coaching opportunities. Landry spent 29 years as the coach of the Dallas Cowboys, recording 20 straight winning seasons between 1966 and 1985. That span included five Super Bowl appearances and two championships. Future NFL coaches Mike Ditka and Dan Reeves were influenced by their time under Landry, having spent time as assistants in Dallas.

COACHING TREES

The lasting influence of NFL coaches can be traced using coaching trees. A coaching tree is like a family tree, except that instead of showing the relationships between family members, it shows how coaches are connected. If a coach served as an assistant under a head coach, those two coaches are linked. Coaching trees can demonstrate the influence of a coach through multiple generations.

Offensive innovator Sid Gillman had a vast influence on the NFL because of his ideas of vertical passing and the coaches he mentored. After a successful career as a college head coach, Gillman coached the Los Angeles Rams

Sid Gillman helped create the modern NFL with his pass-heavy game. He joined the Pro Football Hall of Fame in 1983.

from 1955 to 1959 before jumping to the AFL's San Diego Chargers in 1960. He coached the Chargers through the 1970 merger, spent two years as head coach of the Houston Oilers, and continued in football as an NFL offensive assistant, part of the upstart United States Football League, and a consultant with the University of Pittsburgh in 1987.

Gillman's staff with the Chargers included Chuck Noll, who would later lead the Pittsburgh dynasty of the 1970s, and Al Davis, who would later coach and own the Oakland Raiders. Gillman's reach extends to coaches who worked under Davis and learned his style of passing offense, including Bill Walsh, John Madden, and Tom Flores.

Walsh, influenced by his time as an assistant with the Raiders and Paul Brown's Cincinnati Bengals, developed the West Coast Offense. This style of offense uses quick, high-percentage passes to march an offense down the field. Walsh directed the 49ers to three Super Bowl wins in the 1980s. His offensive style influenced many other coaches.

Paul Brown had been a successful coach at the high school and college level when he was hired to lead the Cleveland team in the newly formed All-American Football Conference. He was so popular in Ohio that a fan vote selected Browns as the team name. His Browns dominated the league and won all four league titles before moving to the NFL after the 1949 season. The success continued as the Browns went to six straight NFL championship games, winning three.

Brown was known as a disciplinarian and implemented several coaching tools still used

> ### MADDEN NFL
>
> Hall of Fame coach John Madden won 103 regular-season games, as well as Super Bowl XI, with the Oakland Raiders. However, today he is probably better known for the video game series that bears his name. The series began in 1988 with *John Madden Football* and changed its name to *Madden NFL* in 1993 when it gained the rights to use all NFL teams and players. The game uses NFL players' names and likenesses with realistic abilities, plays used by the pros, and authentic NFL stadiums. NFL players sometimes get upset over the skill levels assigned to their video-game avatars.

today. His full-time staff worked year round, and he was the first to heavily scout college players. He used tests, classroom teaching techniques, and film study to help his players improve.

Brown was fired in 1962, but he returned to the NFL in 1968 as the first coach of the Cincinnati Bengals, leading them to three playoff appearances in eight years. Brown's influence reaches to Noll, Walsh, Don Shula, and Weeb Ewbank. Ewbank later became the only coach to win NFL and American Football League titles. He coached the Baltimore Colts for nine years, including in "the greatest game ever played," the 1958 NFL championship against the New York Giants. He later coached the New York Jets for 11 years, winning the 1968 AFL title before upsetting his former Colts in Super Bowl III.

PATIENCE IN PITTSBURGH

Some NFL teams are quick to fire a coach after a bad season or two. Pittsburgh has shown more patience, employing a total of three coaches in a 50-year span. Chuck Noll had three losing years before leading the Steelers to four Super Bowl titles in the 1970s. Bill Cowher replaced the retiring Noll in 1992, winning Super Bowl XL and recording 11 winning seasons in 15 years. Mike Tomlin took over in 2007. He won Super Bowl XLIII and had no losing seasons in his first 13 years. "I don't like to criticize other people's way of doing things, but we do feel there's value in stability and continuity, and so that's worked for us," owner Art Rooney II told ESPN in 2016.[1]

CHAPTER 8
THE NFL DRAFT

Commissioner Pete Rozelle works the blackboard during the 1967 NFL Draft.

Bert Bell knew his Philadelphia Eagles had a problem, so he found a solution. Bell, who had founded the Eagles in 1933, struggled to sign new college players to his mediocre team. The best players were signing with the better NFL teams, who could afford to pay more than the league's less successful teams. At an owners' meeting in May 1935, Bell proposed a plan to even out the talented incoming college players across the league.

"I've always had a theory that pro football is like a chain," Bell said at the meeting. "The league is no stronger than its weakest link and I've been a weak link for so long that I should know. Every year the rich get richer and the poor get poorer."[1] Bell's proposal was quickly adopted, and the NFL Draft was born.

Just like the league itself and the Super Bowl, the draft has grown from humble beginnings to become an annual celebration of all things professional football. The first draft was held in February 1936. According to Bell's plan, teams made selections in reverse order of the previous season's finish, picking names from a pool of about 90 eligible college players written on a blackboard at the Ritz-Carlton hotel in Philadelphia.[2] That first draft had nine rounds of picks, and the draft was expanded to 20 rounds in 1939.

The first few drafts were aided by Wellington Mara, son of New York Giants founder Tim Mara. Wellington, a college student, read newspapers and magazines from across the country and created his own unofficial scouting reports, sharing them with all the NFL teams. Teams would later hire full-time staff to do the same thing.

The NFL Draft found competition when the American Football League was formed in 1959. Teams from both leagues were drafting the same players, forcing the young athletes to decide between the NFL and upstart AFL. Heisman Trophy winner Billy Cannon was drafted by the Los Angeles Rams and the Houston Oilers in 1960. He ended up joining the Oilers. Both leagues held secret drafts to prevent the other side from knowing who was selected. The competition created rising salaries, and the leagues agreed to hold a common draft starting in 1967 as part of the merger process.

FINDING THE RIGHT PLAYERS

In 1946, Los Angeles Rams owner Dan Reeves was the first to hire a full-time scout to seek out talent among college seniors. He hired former Packer Eddie Kotal, who would spend much

NUMBER 1 OVERALL PICK

The University of Chicago's Jay Berwanger was the first pick of the first NFL Draft, but he never played in the NFL. Berwanger did everything for his college team and was awarded the first Heisman Trophy in 1935 as the best college football player in the country. The Philadelphia Eagles selected him first in 1936 and traded the rights to the Chicago Bears. Berwanger never accepted the Bears' offer, deciding he could make more money with a full-time job in the business world.

of the year visiting college campuses and games to watch prospects. While many teams used only magazine and newspaper articles to research players, Kotal and Reeves had files on all the eligible players.

NFL teams started to use computers in the 1960s to help track scouting information, but the cost of the technology was too high for many teams. Some teams created alliances to compile and share scouting reports to cut down on the cost of computers, travel, and personnel.

TRADING FOR A DYNASTY

The Dallas Cowboys started the 1989 season 0–5 under first-year coach Jimmy Johnson. Johnson had the idea to trade their best player, running back Herschel Walker, for future draft picks and quickly found a trade partner in Minnesota. The trade, completed on October 12, 1989, became one of the largest and most complicated in NFL history. Dallas sent Walker and three late-round draft picks to Minnesota. Dallas got five veteran players, three picks in the 1990 NFL Draft, including a first-round pick, and conditional picks for future drafts. One of the veteran players refused to come to Dallas and instead got traded to San Diego for two more draft picks.

Johnson used all the picks he gained to make more moves and trades to build his team. He made a total of 51 trades in his five years in Dallas. The Cowboys added key players in this period, including drafting running back Emmitt Smith and safety Darren Woodson.

Walker rushed for 148 yards in his Minnesota debut but did not record another 100-yard game for the Vikings until 1991. Dallas finished the 1989 season 1–15 but had winning records in six of the next seven seasons, along with Super Bowl XXVII, XXVIII, and XXX victories.

Detroit, Philadelphia, and Pittsburgh created the Lions, Eagles and Steelers Talent Organization (LESTO). LESTO was one of three cooperative scouting groups created in the early 1960s. The three scouting groups hosted workouts for prospective players until they decided to merge their events to save money and travel. All 28 NFL teams participated in a workout called the NFL Scouting Combine in 1985, and the event has continued annually since.

THE NFL SCOUTING COMBINE

The NFL Scouting Combine, held in Indianapolis every February since 1987, is like a job interview for college football players. Prospective athletes are invited by the Combine committee to participate in medical evaluations, mental and physical tests, and interviews with NFL team leaders. The workout includes a 40-yard dash, bench press, vertical jump, broad jump, 3-cone drill, and shuttle run, as well as position-related drills. More than 300 athletes participated in 2019, and parts of the workout were shown on the NFL Network and ABC.[3]

AN OFF-SEASON SHOW

The NFL Draft started as a closed-room meeting of NFL owners, but fans started to gain interest in what happened behind the scenes. ESPN president Chet Simmons had the idea in 1979 to broadcast the draft so fans could see what happened when owners and team staff got together. The NFL was surprised anyone would want to watch a business

The modern NFL Draft has become a massive media event.

meeting, but ESPN—still a new cable sports channel—wanted to do something new. "To Pete [Rozelle], it sounded like reading names from the phone book," ESPN anchor Chris Berman said in a 2015 interview with the *Chicago Tribune*. "Everyone said, 'Who's going to watch?'"[4]

ESPN first broadcast the draft in 1980, presenting its morning telecast from a ballroom at the New York Sheraton. The channel added analyst Mel Kiper Jr. in 1984, giving ESPN's coverage the inside knowledge of an experienced scout. The broadcast continued to grow, with a live audience watching the event while millions more watched from home.

The NFL Draft was moved from a morning time slot to the weekend and then, in 2010, to a prime-time extravaganza. ESPN and the NFL Network now cover the event, giving fans an inside look at their teams during the off-season. The 2019 NFL Draft broke records with 600,000 fans attending live while more than 47.5 million viewers watched during the three-day event.[5]

CHAPTER 9

HOME SWEET HOME

Green Bay's Lambeau Field is the oldest stadium that has remained in continuous use by an NFL team.

The NFL-AFL merger sent several of the professional football teams scrambling for new homes. One of the policies as the leagues came together was that all NFL teams had to play in a stadium with a capacity of at least 50,000 by 1970.[1] The Kansas City Chiefs, Dallas Cowboys, and Boston Patriots (which later became the New England Patriots) all built new stadiums. The Chicago Bears were able to comply by moving across town.

The Bears spent most of their early history playing at Wrigley Field before moving to Soldier Field in 1971. The Patriots found room outside of Boston and built a new home in Foxborough, Massachusetts, for the 1971 season before replacing it in 2002 with their current home, Gillette Stadium. Dallas and Kansas City each built new stadiums in the early 1970s to meet the capacity rule and set the standard for football-first stadiums.

HISTORIC HOMES

The Los Angeles Memorial Coliseum opened in 1923 as the home of the University of Southern California Trojans and has since hosted two Super Bowls, two Olympic Games, one World Series, and three NFL teams. The Coliseum was the home of the Los Angeles Dons, an All-American Football Conference team, in the 1940s, before it became the home of the Rams, the Raiders, and briefly the Chargers. The Rams moved from Saint Louis back to the Coliseum in 2016 while they waited for a new stadium to be built in nearby Inglewood. The Coliseum was chosen to host Super Bowl I and later saw the 1972 Dolphins cap their perfect season with a win in Super Bowl VII. The Coliseum's iconic east entrance features the Olympic torch, Olympic rings, and life-size bronze statues of male and female athletes.

Soldier Field opened in 1924, hosting college football games. It was also the home to the Chicago Cardinals for one year in 1959. The Bears moved to Soldier Field in 1971 and have stayed, although the stadium underwent major reconstruction in 2002. The city of Chicago decided to redo the inside of the stadium rather than let the team move to a new location. The historic exterior of the stadium, featuring a series of Greek-inspired columns and walkways, was kept while the interior was updated.

NAMING RIGHTS

Companies like AT&T, MetLife Insurance, and Mercedes-Benz spend anywhere from $3 million to $20 million a year to have an NFL stadium named after them, giving them advertising every time fans go to or talk about the stadium.[2]

Some NFL organizations have resisted putting a corporate name on their stadiums. Green Bay's Lambeau Field and Cincinnati's Paul Brown Stadium continue to bear the names of their organizations' famous coaches. Chicago's Soldier Field took its name in 1925 as a memorial to American soldiers who have died in combat. Lamar Hunt named the Kansas City Chiefs' home Arrowhead Stadium when it opened in 1972.

LEAPING IN LAMBEAU

As Green Bay safety LeRoy Butler raced to the end zone for a defensive touchdown during a 1993 home game, he saw fans cheering just behind the end zone. He decided to join them, leaping onto the wall to hug the first row of Packer fans. The Lambeau Leap has become a tradition in Green Bay for players who score, and it's not flagged by the NFL as excessive celebration. A statue has been added outside the stadium where fans can leap onto a short wall with four bronze fans. It sits near statues of famous coaches Vince Lombardi and Curly Lambeau.

Lambeau Field was the first stadium built specifically for an NFL team. The Green Bay Packers played at City Stadium beginning in the 1920s and played some games at County Stadium in Milwaukee. The NFL threatened to move the team to Milwaukee permanently if Green Bay didn't offer a new stadium to replace the 25,000-capacity City Stadium. The new stadium opened with 32,000 seats in 1957, was named after team founder Curly Lambeau in 1965, and has been expanded several times. The historic stadium now has a capacity of more than 80,000, making it one of the largest in the league.[3]

STATE-OF-THE-ART STADIUMS

The Dallas Cowboys kicked off the age of super stadiums with the first $1-billion facility, AT&T Stadium. The structure opened in 2009 to replace Texas Stadium, where the Cowboys had played for nearly 40 years. AT&T Stadium features a retractable roof and giant retractable glass doors at each end zone. The 100,000-capacity stadium also has a massive video board hanging 90 feet (27 m) above midfield and stretching from one 25-yard line to the other.[4]

The Minnesota Vikings opened the $1.1-billion US Bank Stadium in 2016 with several unique and advanced features. The stadium's slanted roof is partially transparent, allowing natural light to fill the 66,200-capacity building. Fans are

GAME DAY EXTRAS

Some NFL stadiums have extra surprises to enhance fans' experiences. Special features and events at these stadiums make their games unique in the league. Jacksonville's TIAA Bank Field features a party deck in the north end zone that has two pools and 20 cabanas with outdoor furniture.[5] The Jaguars added the league's first in-stadium dog park in 2018, allowing fans to bring their dogs to play during games.

In New England, the End Zone Militia, a group of 20 reenactors dressed in authentic clothing of the 1700s, fires their muskets every time the Patriots score at Gillette Stadium. In Tampa Bay, Raymond James Stadium's main feature is Buccaneer Cove, an area behind the north end zone that looks like a pirate village from the 1800s. It also has a replica pirate ship that shoots eight cannons when the home team scores a touchdown.

Seattle recognized fans at CenturyLink Field by retiring the number 12 in honor of their "12th man," a nickname for the support the team gets from the home crowd. A local celebrity raises the special 12th Man Flag before every home game. In Pittsburgh, fans wave their Terrible Towels at Heinz Field to support the Steelers.

The innovative roof of Mercedes-Benz Stadium lets the facility easily transition between indoor and outdoor play.

greeted by a 160-foot (49 m) Viking ship with a giant LED video board for its sail near the main entrance. That side of the building also has five 95-foot- (29 m) high pivoting glass doors that allow for views of Minneapolis as well as the chance to let in fresh air during good weather.[6]

Mercedes-Benz Stadium opened in Atlanta a year later at a cost of $1.5 billion. It features a retractable roof that is also translucent, allowing natural light in when it's open or closed. The unique retractable roof opens with eight triangular pieces that look like a pinwheel as they slide open. The stadium features a giant halo-shaped video board as well as a support column behind one end zone that is covered with more video boards. The column can also be seen from outside the stadium through floor-to-ceiling windows that show off downtown Atlanta. A 41.5-foot (12.6 m) stainless steel falcon statue stands guard outside the 71,000-seat arena.[7] These three new stadiums have each hosted a Super Bowl since opening.

CHAPTER 10
NFL CONTROVERSIES

Hard hits, which can cause injuries including concussions, have drawn controversy to the NFL in recent years. ▶

The NFL has had its share of controversies and challenges. Passionate fan bases get upset when a call doesn't go their team's way, especially when referees or poorly written rules are to blame. Fan bases have also been shocked when their hometown team decides to leave suddenly for a new city and a new stadium.

The league has also been rocked by scandals as athletes and owners with egos, fame, and money have drawn attention to their off-the-field actions. The NFL has had to navigate drug problems and criminal issues among its players. Other controversies have to do with the violent nature of the game itself. Player safety and the long-term effects of concussions have made major headlines for the NFL.

AL DAVIS VS. THE NFL

Al Davis became coach of the Oakland Raiders in 1963 before becoming commissioner of the AFL in 1966. Davis's leadership led to the competition between leagues for football players. This eventually led to the merger. Other owners met about the merger in secret to avoid Davis, and Pete Rozelle remained commissioner of the new NFL.

When NFL owners voted against the Raiders' move to Los Angeles in 1980, Davis sued the league and won. He later sided with the USFL in its suit against the NFL in 1986. The Raiders moved back to Oakland, but Davis threatened other moves and more lawsuits. The NFL passed a rule in 1997 stating that franchises that sue the league and lose would have to pay the NFL's legal fees.

CONCUSSIONS AND CTE

Injuries have long been a part of football. Concussions—brain injuries resulting from hard impacts to the head—have become much more widely recognized in the modern NFL. Many have argued that the league did not do enough to protect or educate players until retired NFL players began showing symptoms of the long-term effects of concussions. Dr. Bennet Omalu discovered a degenerative brain disorder linked to repeated brain injuries when he did an autopsy on Hall of Fame player Mike Webster in 2002. Omalu called the disorder chronic traumatic encephalopathy (CTE).

Webster played for Pittsburgh for 15 years, but life after football was hard. He was diagnosed with brain damage in 1999 and struggled with depression, homelessness, memory loss, and erratic behavior. He died of a heart attack in 2002, and Omalu researched Webster's brain for three years before releasing a paper on the subject. The NFL disagreed with Omalu's finding until several more cases of CTE were diagnosed after the deaths of former players.

Many retired players have reported the same symptoms as Webster, including erratic behavior and suicidal thoughts. Several players asked their families to donate their brains to science to further CTE research. Some have died by suicide. Former players, including Super Bowl XXVI MVP Mark Rypien, and their families sued the NFL in 2012 over concussions. Rypien later said he believed he had brain damage leading to erratic and sometimes violent behavior. The class action lawsuit was settled in 2015, with the NFL paying up to $5 million to retired players for conditions associated with brain injuries.[1]

Removing injury from the game entirely is not possible, but the NFL has taken steps to reduce the chance of serious brain injuries. It made rule changes to ban head-to-head hits and reduce the likelihood of head-on collisions between players during kickoffs. It also enforced a new

CONCUSSION PROTOCOL

The NFL has rules in place for the treatment of players with concussions and penalties for teams who do not follow the concussion protocol. The protocol says players with possible concussions should be immediately removed from the field. The team physician and an unaffiliated neurotrauma consultant perform an examination of the player. The player is taken to the locker room for a complete assessment if there is any suspicion of a concussion, and any player diagnosed with a concussion cannot return to play. If a player passes the examination, he will be closely monitored.

The league has a list of observable symptoms, including loss of consciousness, vacant looks, or disorientation. Spotters at each game look for these symptoms. There is also a protocol to clear players returning from a concussion. The five-step process includes rest until signs and symptoms of the concussion have passed and the player passes a neurologic examination, light aerobic exercise, the addition of strength training, participation in non-contact drills and team meetings, and finally full practice. NFL data shows that reported concussions fell from 281 during the 2017 season to 214 in 2018. However, more than 200 concussions were reported in each season between 2012 and 2018.[2]

concussion protocol for injured players starting in 2016, with the goal of ensuring that players who suffer a concussion in the middle of a game do not return to the game and worsen their injury.

ON-FIELD CONTROVERSIES

Some fans still argue the Immaculate Reception and the Music City Miracle were not legal plays. Another controversial call, known as the Holy Roller, occurred in 1978. Raiders quarterback Ken Stabler purposely fumbled forward to avoid a sack. Two more Raider players pushed the ball forward before one fell on it in the end zone for a touchdown. It was a legal play at the time, but the rule was soon changed.

Another rule interpretation led to the so-called Tuck Rule Game in the 2001 AFC divisional playoff. New England quarterback Tom Brady was sacked and seemingly fumbled late in the game. The call was overturned because of the tuck rule, which called it an incomplete pass if the quarterback was tucking the ball into his body in the process of a throw. The Patriots kept the ball, beat Oakland in that playoff game, and went on to win the first Super Bowl of the Brady-Belichick era. The tuck rule was removed from the NFL rulebook in 2013.

Rule changes on the definition of a catch have also confused players, fans, and referees. Tampa Bay's Bert

Determining what makes a legal catch has been an issue of confusion and frustration for fans.

Emanuel had a diving catch overturned late in the 1999 NFC Championship Game. He secured the football with both hands before falling on top of the ball. The ball touched the ground, but he never lost control. It was initially ruled a catch, giving the Buccaneers a chance at continuing the late drive. But it was overturned after officials viewed the replay, because the rulebook said if any part of the football touched the ground it was incomplete. The rulebook was changed that off-season and has been edited several times since.

OTHER PROBLEMS

The NFL has had to deal with player behavior off the field, including domestic violence and other criminal acts. The league reviews incidents and has instituted a six-game suspension for first-time offenders of domestic violence.

Former Baltimore running back Ray Rice was suspended for two games during the 2014 season after hitting his then-fiancée Janay Palmer. Criminal charges were dropped, but Rice was suspended indefinitely when a video of him punching Palmer was released. Rice was released by Baltimore and has not played in the NFL since.

Teams have also gotten in trouble with the league. The Patriots were caught videotaping an opponent's hand signals in 2007, and Tom Brady was accused of intentionally deflating footballs for a better grip during the 2014 playoffs. New Orleans had several coaches suspended in 2012 when it was discovered the team paid bonuses for injuring opposing players.

San Francisco quarterback Colin Kaepernick started protesting by kneeling during the National Anthem before games in 2016, trying to draw attention to racial issues. Many other players followed, seeking to protest police brutality, racism, or other issues. Some NFL fans became upset, and the league's viewership dropped that season. Kaepernick became a free agent and could not find a new team in 2017. The NFL created a policy in 2018 to prevent protests, stating athletes should remain in the locker room if they do not want to stand for the National Anthem. However, it decided not to discipline athletes in violation of the rule.

THE NFL AND COVID-19

In early 2020, a new disease called COVID-19 swept the globe, leaving millions infected and hundreds of thousands dead. To slow its spread, health officials instructed people to maintain physical distance between each other. This had a dramatic impact on the NFL. Though its regular season begins in September, off-season activities were affected by the pandemic. Team training activities were delayed. The NFL Draft went ahead in late April, though it happened virtually. NFL commissioner Roger Goodell hosted the draft from his basement. "We're planning on playing this fall even though it may be different," he said.[3]

THE EXCITEMENT CONTINUES

Despite the league's controversies, the NFL's popularity has remained high. NFL viewership increased in 2018 and 2019 after going down some during the National Anthem controversy.

Excitement built for the latest NFL headlines, such as the Raiders' move to a brand-new stadium in Las Vegas or the Rams' and Chargers' new home in Los Angeles. The success of the NFL's overseas games in London may lead to a full-time franchise outside of the United States. The NFL says London has the fan interest, government support, and quality stadiums to possibly one day host a franchise.

Young stars like quarterback Patrick Mahomes continue to make the NFL exciting to watch more than a century after the league's debut.

Most important is the weekly product on the field. The NFL's big names, from veteran stars like Brady and Brees to younger players like Mahomes, Deshaun Watson and Saquon Barkley, create must-watch moments. Every game matters as teams battle for the ultimate goal—a chance to play in the Super Bowl. The NFL's championship game is basically a national holiday when the attention of much of the country turns to the league. After 100 years, the NFL still excites fans across the United States and the world.

ESSENTIAL FACTS

Significant Events

- Professional football became organized in 1920 when representatives from several Midwest teams formed the American Professional Football Association. The league changed its name to the National Football League in 1922.

- The American Football League was founded in 1959 as a rival to the NFL. The eight-team league featured a more exciting brand of football.

- The two leagues caused skyrocketing salaries as they fought over the top players, so a merger was proposed. The proposal included a championship game between the two leagues in 1966 before the ten AFL teams joined the 16 NFL teams to create the modern NFL.

- The merger created the Super Bowl, which has grown into one of the biggest annual sporting events. Millions of viewers tune in for the game, creative commercials, and concert-like halftime show.

- Tom Flores became the first minority coach to win a Super Bowl when he led Oakland to two titles. Tony Dungy became the first African American head coach to lift the Lombardi Trophy, leading Indianapolis past Lovie Smith's Chicago Bears in Super Bowl XLI.

Key Players

- New England Patriots quarterback Tom Brady has been named the league's most valuable player three times and has the most career wins of any quarterback.

- Kansas City Chiefs quarterback Patrick Mahomes was named the NFL's most valuable player after throwing 50 touchdown passes during the 2018 season. He led the Chiefs to a victory in Super Bowl LIV.

- Pittsburgh Steelers rookie running back Franco Harris grabbed a tipped pass just before it hit the ground and raced down the sideline for a game-winning touchdown in a playoff game. The Immaculate Reception is one of the NFL's most iconic moments.

- The offensive trio of quarterback Troy Aikman, running back Emmitt Smith, and receiver Michael Irvin led the Dallas Cowboys to three Super Bowl victories in a four-year span.

Key Teams

- The Miami Dolphins went undefeated in 1972. They won all 14 regular-season games before capping a perfect 17–0 season with a win in Super Bowl VII.

- The Pittsburgh Steelers dominated the NFL in the 1970s. They won four Super Bowls in that decade.

- Coach Bill Belichick has led the New England Patriots to 17 AFC East Division titles and six Super Bowl wins.

- The Green Bay Packers won six league titles between 1929 and 1944, including three after the addition of a championship game. They won three more NFL titles and the first two Super Bowls in the 1960s under coach Vince Lombardi.

Quote

"[Commissioner Pete Rozelle] moved the NFL from the back page to the front page. From daytime to prime time."

—*New York Giants owner Wellington Mara*

GLOSSARY

broadcast
To transmit a program by radio or television.

commissioner
A person appointed to regulate a particular sport.

controversial
Giving rise or likely to give rise to public disagreement.

debut
A person's first appearance in a specific role.

dynasty
An extended period of excellence or success for a team.

expansion
The addition of a new team to a league.

franchise
A professional sports team that is part of a league.

free agent
A player whose rights are not owned by any team.

iconic
Having the characteristics of someone or something that is very famous or popular.

interception
A pass intended for an offensive player that is caught by a defensive player.

merger
The act of combining two or more organizations to create a single, larger one.

monopoly
Exclusive control over a commodity or service.

overtime
Extra time played at the end of a game that is tied at the end of regulation time.

prominence
The state of being leading, important, or well known.

prospect
An athlete likely to succeed at the next level.

retractable
Able to be drawn back or back in.

rookie
An athlete in his or her first full season in a sport.

strike
A workers' protest that involves refusing to work until requests are met.

sudden death
A situation in which the first team to score will automatically win the game.

turnover
When one team loses possession of the ball to the other team.

upset
To unexpectedly beat a team or player who was heavily favored to win.

veteran
A player who has played many years in the league.

ADDITIONAL RESOURCES

Selected Bibliography

Gifford, Frank, and Peter Richmond. *The Glory Game: How the 1958 NFL Championship Changed Football Forever.* Harper, 2008.

Horrigan, Joe. *NFL Century: The One-Hundred-Year Rise of America's Greatest Sports League.* Crown, 2019.

Willis, Chris. *The Man Who Built the National Football League.* Scarecrow Press, 2010.

Further Readings

Harris, Duchess, JD, PhD, and Cynthia Kennedy Henzel. *Politics and Protest in Sports.* Abdo, 2019.

Monson, James. *Patrick Mahomes: NFL Sensation.* Abdo, 2020.

Watson, Stephanie. *Brain Injuries in Football.* Abdo, 2015.

Online Resources

To learn more about the NFL, please visit **abdobooklinks.com** or scan this QR code. These links are routinely monitored and updated to provide the most current information available.

More Information

For more information on this subject, contact or visit the following organizations:

National Football League Headquarters
345 Park Ave.
New York, NY 10154
800-635-5300
nfl.com

The main office of the NFL, which oversees the league business, is located in New York City.

Pro Football Hall of Fame
Pro Football Hall of Fame
2121 George Halas Dr. NW
Canton, OH 44708
330-456-8207
profootballhof.com

The Pro Football Hall of Fame includes a museum dedicated to the history of professional football and its greatest players. It includes interactive displays and busts of those inducted to the Hall of Fame.

Wilson Football Factory
217 N. Liberty St.
Ada, OH 45810
419-634-9901
wilson.com/en-us/explore/football/ada-ohio-factory

This factory is dedicated to making footballs, including the ones used in the Super Bowl. Fans can take a tour of the factory.

SOURCE NOTES

CHAPTER 1. THIS IS THE NFL

1. Mike Triplett. "Sean Payton: Saints Will 'Never Get Over' Blown Pass Interference Call." *ESPN*, 20 Jan. 2019, espn.com. Accessed 27 Jan. 2020.

2. "Patriots Make 3rd Straight Super Bowl, Beat Chiefs 37–31 OT." *ESPN*, 20 Jan. 2019, espn.com. Accessed 27 Jan. 2020.

CHAPTER 2. THE LEAGUE'S ORIGINS

1. Joe F. Carr and Chris Willis. *The Man Who Built the National Football League*. The Scarecrow Press, 2010. 123.

2. Jerry Tapp. "NFL Census: Data on Players' Race, Weight & Height." *Heavy*, 24 Sept. 2014, heavy.com. Accessed 27 Jan. 2020.

3. "Greatest Game Ever Played." *Pro Football Hall of Fame*, 2020, profootballhof.com. Accessed 27 Jan. 2020.

4. "The 100 Greatest Moments in Sports History: The Guarantee." *Sports Illustrated*, n.d., si.com. Accessed 27 Jan. 2020.

CHAPTER 3. THE NFL BECOMES AMERICA'S FAVORITE

1. Bob Carter. "Rozelle Made NFL What It Is Today." *ESPN*, n.d., espn.com. Accessed 27 Jan. 2020.

2. "Miami's Perfect Season." *Pro Football Hall of Fame*, 2020, profootballhof.com. Accessed 27 Jan. 2020.

3. Adam Stites. "The Brief History of NFL Mexico Games." *SBNation*, 18 Nov. 2019, sbnation.com. Accessed 27 Jan. 2020.

4. "Giants vs. Dolphins - Game Summary." *ESPN*, 28 Oct. 2007, espn.com. Accessed 27 Jan. 2020.

5. Kevin Seifert. "Flowing Streams: NFL Ratings up on Digital, TV." *ESPN*, 11 Sept. 2019, espn.com. Accessed 27 Jan. 2020.

CHAPTER 4. THE PLAYOFFS' GREATEST MOMENTS

1. "The Ice Bowl." *Pro Football Hall of Fame*, 2020, profootballhof.com. Accessed 27 Jan. 2020.

2. Bill Syken. *Sports Illustrated Football's Greatest*. Sports Illustrated Books, 2012. 176.

3. "Staubach, Pearson Discuss Genesis of 'Hail Mary' Pass." *Dallas Morning News*, 17 Jan. 2010, dallasnews.com. Accessed 27 Jan. 2020.

CHAPTER 5. THE SUPER BOWL

1. "Corny and a Bit Presumptuous, But It's Still the 'Super Bowl.'" *St. Petersburg Times*, 7 Jan. 1970, news.google.com. Accessed 27 Jan. 2020.

2. "Super Bowl LIII Draws 98.2 Million TV Viewers, 32.3 Million Social Media Interactions." *Nielsen*, 4 Feb. 2019, nielsen.com. Accessed 27 Jan. 2020.

3. Tom Huddleston Jr. "This Is How Much It Costs to Air a Commercial During the 2019 Super Bowl." *CNBC*, 30 Jan. 2019, cnbc.com. Accessed 27 Jan. 2020.

4. "Super Bowl Average Costs of a 30-Second TV Advertisement from 2002 to 2019 (in Million U.S. Dollars)." *Statista*, 9 Aug. 2019, statista.com. Accessed 27 Jan. 2020.

5. Jorge Milian. "Remembering Super Bowl V: Baltimore Colts' Jim O'Brien Got a Win and a Future Wife." *Palm Beach Post*, 31 Mar. 2012, palmbeachpost.com. Accessed 27 Jan. 2020.

6. "Super Bowl LIII Draws 98.2 Million TV Viewers."

CHAPTER 6. NFL DYNASTIES

1. Jeré Longman. "Eagles' 1960 Victory Was an N.F.L. Turning Point." *New York Times*, 6 Jan. 2011, nytimes.com. Accessed 27 Jan. 2020.

CHAPTER 7. COACHING LEGENDS

1. Jeremy Fowler. "Steelers' Unmatched Coaching Longevity the Envy of NFL Peers." *ESPN*, 24 Mar. 2016, espn.com. Accessed 27 Jan. 2020.

SOURCE NOTES CONTINUED

CHAPTER 8. THE NFL DRAFT

1. Joe F. Carr and Chris Willis. *The Man Who Built the National Football League*. The Scarecrow Press, 2010. 338–343.

2. Carr and Willis, *The Man Who Built the National Football League*, 338–343.

3. Neil Reynolds. "What Is the NFL Scouting Combine?" *NFL*, 20 Feb. 2019, nfl.com. Accessed 27 Jan. 2020.

4. Ed Sherman. "ESPN's Chris Berman Has Seen NFL Draft's Popularity Soar." *Chicago Tribune*, 26 Apr. 2015, chicagotribune.com. Accessed 27 Jan. 2020.

5. "Record Nashville Crowd Hosts Most-Watched Draft." *NFL*, 29 Apr. 2019, nfl.com. Accessed 27 Jan. 2020.

CHAPTER 9. HOME SWEET HOME

1. Hayden Bird. "Remembering the AFL-NFL Merger 50 Years Ago." *Boston*, 9 June 2016, boston.com. Accessed 27 Jan. 2020.

2. Kristi Dosh. "New NFL Stadium in Inglewood Reportedly Lands Naming Rights Deal with Social Finance." *Forbes*, 29 May 2019, forbes.com. Accessed 27 Jan. 2020.

3. "Lambeau Field." *Stadiums of Pro Football*, 2019, stadiumsofprofootball.com. Accessed 27 Jan. 2020.

4. "AT&T Stadium." *Stadiums of Pro Football*, 2019, stadiumsofprofootball.com. Accessed 27 Jan. 2020.

5. "TIAA Bank Field." *Stadiums of Pro Football*, 2019, stadiumsofprofootball.com. Accessed 27 Jan. 2020.

6. "US Bank Stadium." *Stadiums of Pro Football*, 2019, stadiumsofprofootball.com. Accessed 27 Jan. 2020.

7. "Mercedes-Benz Stadium." *Stadiums of Pro Football*, 2019, stadiumsofprofootball.com. Accessed 27 Jan. 2020.

CHAPTER 10. NFL CONTROVERSIES

1. "NFL, Ex-players Agree to $765M Settlement in Concussions Suit." *NFL*, 29 Aug. 2013, nfl.com. Accessed 27 Jan. 2020.

2. Brian Resnick. "What a Lifetime of Playing Football Can Do to the Human Brain." *Vox*, 3 Feb. 2019, vox.com. Accessed 27 Jan. 2020.

3. Elizabeth Elkind. "NFL Commissioner Roger Goodell Expects 2020 Season Will Be 'On Time' but It May Be 'Different.'" *CBS News*, 24 Apr. 2020, cbsnews.com. Accessed 28 Apr. 2020.

INDEX

All-American Football Conference, 19, 57, 72, 84
American Football League (AFL), 21–23, 31, 39, 46, 71, 73, 77, 84, 92
American Professional Football Association (APFA), 16, 17, 18
AT&T Stadium, 85, 86–87

Belichick, Bill, 56, 68, 95
Bell, Bert, 19, 76
Berman, Chris, 80
Berwanger, Jay, 77
Brady, Tom, 9–12, 51, 52, 56, 65, 68, 95, 97, 99
Brees, Drew, 6–8, 11, 65, 99
Brown, Paul, 19, 72–73, 85
Burkhead, Rex, 10–11

Carr, Joe, 17–18
Catch, The, 41–42, 50, 61
CenturyLink Field, 87
Chamberlin, Guy, 69
Christmas Day games, 38
chronic traumatic encephalopathy (CTE), 93
Clark, Dwight, 41–42
Cleveland Browns, 19, 20, 26, 29, 30, 35, 57, 72
coaching trees, 70
college football, 16, 18, 50, 60, 68, 70, 72, 73, 76–79, 85
concussions, 92–95
controversial calls, 6, 7, 9, 95–96
COVID-19, 98

Dallas Cowboys, 22, 27, 35, 56, 63, 70, 78, 84, 86
Davis, Al, 29, 71, 92
digital streaming, 31
domestic violence, 97
Dungy, Tony, 69

Elway, John, 49, 51
Ewbank, Weeb, 73
expansion teams, 21, 29

Flores, Tom, 64, 69, 71

Gillette Stadium, 84, 87
Gillman, Sid, 70–71
Goff, Jared, 7, 11
Grange, Harold "Red," 18
Green Bay Packers, 18, 23, 35, 39–40, 57, 69, 86

Hail Mary passes, 42
Halas, George, 68–69
Hay, Ralph, 16
Hunt, Lamar, 21–22, 46, 47, 85

Ice Bowl, the, 39
Immaculate Reception, the, 40–41, 61, 95
international games, 27–29

Johnson, Jimmy, 78

Kaepernick, Colin, 97
Kiper, Mel, Jr., 81

Lambeau, Curly, 68, 69, 86
Lambeau Field, 39, 85–86
Landry, Tom, 27, 70
Lombardi, Vince, 57, 69–70, 86
Los Angeles Memorial Coliseum, 29, 84–85

Madden, John, 64, 69, 71, 72
Mahomes, Patrick, 6, 9–11, 99
Mara, Wellington, 26, 76
Mercedes-Benz Stadium, 85, 89
Miami Dolphins, 26–28, 34, 35, 38, 64, 85
Monday Night Football, 26
Montana, Joe, 41–42, 48–49, 50, 61, 63
most valuable player (MVP), 9, 11, 23, 50, 58, 61, 62, 63, 64, 93
Music City Miracle, the, 42–43

Namath, Joe, 22, 23
National Anthem protests, 97–98
New England Patriots, 6, 9–12, 35, 51–52, 56, 68, 84, 87, 95, 97
NFL Draft, 13, 50, 60, 62, 76–81
NFL Europe, 28–29
NFL Network, 26, 31, 79, 81
NFL Scouting Combine, 79
NFL-AFL merger, 22–23, 26, 27, 33, 46, 77, 84, 92
1958 NFL Championship Game, 20–21
Noll, Chuck, 58, 71, 73

Oakland Raiders, 29–30, 40, 58, 64, 69, 71, 72, 84, 92, 95, 98
O'Brien, Jim, 49
Omalu, Bennett, 93

Payton, Sean, 6, 7, 68
Pittsburgh Steelers, 27, 33, 35, 40, 58, 61, 73, 79, 87
playoffs, 6–12, 13, 26, 32, 38–43, 48, 56, 58, 60, 61, 63, 64, 68, 73, 95, 97
Pollard, Fritz, 69

relocations, 29–31
Rice, Jerry, 60, 63
Rozelle, Pete, 26, 31, 32, 46, 80, 92
rulebook, 94–96
Rypien, Mark, 58, 93

Schramm, Tex, 22
scouting, 62, 68, 73, 76–79, 81
Shell, Art, 69
Smith, Emmitt, 62, 63–64, 65, 78
Soldier Field, 84, 85
stadiums, 29, 30, 46, 72, 84–89, 98
Starr, Bart, 39, 58
strikes, 26, 32, 58
Super Bowl, 6, 9, 11–13, 23, 26–27, 33, 38–39, 42, 46–53, 56–58, 60–64, 68–70, 72, 73, 76, 78, 84–85, 89, 93, 95, 99

television, 20, 26, 31, 34, 46–48
Thorpe, Jim, 16
TIAA Bank Field, 87
trades, 50, 52, 77, 78
Tuck Rule, 95

Unitas, Johnny, 20, 21, 49
United States Football League (USFL), 34, 92
US Bank Stadium, 87

Walker, Herschel, 34, 78
Washington Redskins, 35, 58
Webster, Mike, 93
World Football League (WFL), 33–34

XFL, 34

Young, Steve, 34, 63

ABOUT THE AUTHOR

Tom Glave

Tom Glave learned to write about sports at the University of Missouri. He has written about sports for newspapers in New Jersey, Missouri, Arkansas, and Texas. He has also written several books about sports. He looks forward to teaching Tommy, Lucas, Allison, and Olivia all about sports.